Glitter Ball

Ellen Lorenzi-Prince

TYBORNE HILL PUBLISHERS
WEST LONG BRANCH NEW JERSEY

Tyborne Hill Publishers
55 Locust Avenue
West Long Branch, New Jersey
Visit our website at www.tybornehill.com

Editor: *Audrey DeLaMartre*

Cover Design and Photography: *Sophie Lorenzi-Prince*

ISBN: 978-0-9776326-7-1

Printed in the United States of America

Glitter Ball

Spring

Dancing Queen

Hot water beat on her neck, and streamed down her naked back. The near scalding made Lisa feel real again, after a day of saying words the hotel put into her mouth. To be herself again, after hours of strangers calling her by a name they read on a badge, then smirking as if they knew her. The shower brought her back to life. She must be real, if so much water couldn't wash her away.

If it weren't for Claire, she thought as she dried off, *she wouldn't stay at that job another day.* But the day was done. The week of days was done! It was Friday night. Time to get ready for the time of her life.

She stared at her face in the mirror. A blank young woman stared back. Back in Colorado, makeup was a vanity, something bad girls wore, and she'd felt guilty sneaking a bit of lipstick. But Lisa lived in New Orleans now and times had changed.

Besides check-in procedures, Claire taught her about makeup. Claire told her she was attractive, and the right makeup would show everybody.

Lisa smoothed on foundation, to start with an even mask. Then she decorated it: enough blusher for the cheeks to look hot and sculpted under uncertain light, lavender frosting on the eyelids, glossy pink on the lips. Bright and shiny meant beautiful in 1978.

She paused before the crucial step. Mascara. When each layer went on seamlessly, that meant she'd have a good night. If she ran out of clean fingers from wiping it off her skin, that was a bad sign.

She was going to have a good night. She knew it. She smiled at her reflection; it was quite pretty now. They wouldn't know her back home.

Because she was meant to be here, where happiness might sparkle in her hands like diamonds. She'd found a job, she'd found an apartment, and she'd found Claire. And Claire had brought her to Promises.

She wished Claire were coming tonight. But Claire had a date with Charlie. Lisa shuddered. She didn't often like the men Claire dated. None of them adored Claire as they ought. But Charlie was downright creepy. It was like she could never get a good look at his face. No matter the light, it was always in shadow.

She was cold. Time she put on a dress. It had to be a good night. It had to be her favorite dress. White like a bride, and shimmering like angel wings, but the way it clung to her breasts and hips suggested something far less innocent. The bows on her shoulders were girlish, but one tug on them might undress her completely. Her body would whisper, "I'm so naked under here," beneath her serious sweet eyes. A killer combination, Claire said.

Still she couldn't dress like this, except for the makeup. But it went with the face she created, and the part she meant to play, the role of the dancing queen.

She strapped on platform sandals and she was ready. She wanted to dance. She wanted to dance! She felt it like an itch in her feet, her hands, her belly. But it was too early to make her entrance. Girls who went this early were looking for a guy who'd spend more than one night with them. She wasn't one of those girls.

She sat on the edge of her bed and listened to classical music to stay calm. She would not give herself to a pulsing beat until she sought it at the source, at the disco. She breathed and imagined Vienna woods.

When she returned, she was pleased. It was ten minutes past the earliest she allowed herself to leave. She stood up. Her heart raced already.

Throwing open her door, Lisa nearly ran into her new neighbor across the hall.

"Hi, Lisa. Wow, you look fantastic! You're going dancing again?"

Jess worked at the diner down the street. Her uniform was hideous, much worse than Lisa's, and got sweaty, stained and pawed at. But Jess flashed a genuine smile. The ugliness didn't seem to get her down. Lisa wondered how she managed that.

"Thanks! I am," Lisa said. "You should come with me sometime. It'd be fun."

"Oh, I'd love to. I love to dance. If I wasn't so dead tired… But all I want now is to put my feet up and watch TV."

"Maybe another night?"

"I'm off tomorrow, but I'm going out with Pete," said Jess. Pete was a cook at the diner. "He's not much for dancing. We'll probably go play pool."

Jess shrugged and laughed. Lisa smiled with her, but shook her head as she turned away. Not to dance when you wanted to, needed to—you might as well be back in Colorado. Or back in the bayous, in Jess's case.

"Another time, then," she said.

Lisa pulled up to Promises and parked. An elegant Southern townhouse, all pastel paint, arched windows and French doors, like any other in this genteel uptown neighborhood. But the others didn't have chaos spilling from them. She could feel the throb of the music from her car. How the people on the sidewalk could laugh as if they were deaf to its rhythm was beyond her.

Stepping inside, the beat body-slammed her. She nodded to the doorman, Steve, and to Wendy, sitting beside him. Wendy, the daytime bartender, was usually gone by now, but Lisa did not stop to wonder. She had to move.

Past the dark velvet wallpaper, the great gilded mirrors, and rich antique furniture. Threading through the crowd and the smoke to the back. The business end was up front: the backgammon playing, drink selling, and partner negotiating. The sex, the dancing and groping, took place in the back. Above Promise's parquet dance floor hung the great revolving ball. The glittered stream that turned faces ecstatic and movements spasmodic and final. She took a deep breath, lifted her chin, and swept her way to the far end of the bar.

"Hi, Tommy," Lisa said to the bartender.

"Hello, darlin'. You look gorgeous as ever. The usual?"

"Yes, please." Lisa put a few dollars on the bar. Within seconds Tommy replaced it with a glass of white wine and some change. One more smile just for her from his black lashed green eyes, and he moved on to the next customer. Lisa liked Tommy. His compliments hadn't stopped when she'd refused him, but his propositions had.

She always bought herself a drink right off, so a guy couldn't use that as an excuse for conversation. She wasn't here to talk.

She gazed steadily at the dance floor. She let her body move a little in place, a tiny tap of the foot, a gentle sway of the hips. It was obvious what she wanted. She'd prepared her part; she waited for a man to come play his.

A man came. He asked her to dance. She'd danced with him before, as a warm-up. She didn't remember his name. She'd never told him hers. But they knew each other. He knew a dance was all he'd get. He hoped for more from the other girls; there might be one who would go home with him, one who might look at him twice if he had another pretty girl on his arm.

He wasn't great, but he didn't embarrass her. He didn't pay her much attention. Lisa was glad of that. The rhythm beat on her, not in her. Her brain moved her feet. She ached for the song to move her feet for her instead. She closed her eyes.

She and he danced, and parted companionably. She sipped her wine and waited. She didn't have to wait long.

"Hi. My name's Mark." A slow cool voice, with an uptown accent. Lisa turned to see the good-looking guy she'd noticed last week, without the other girl on his arm. "Lisa," she replied.

She looked him up and down, but blushed prettily when caught, as if he had not been doing the same to her. His grin was huge.

He led her out to the dance floor, his hand light on the small of her back. She loved the manners of a Southern gentleman. His hand was warm, radiant. The blood rushed away from her head. This could be it. A fast dance number rolled out from the speakers. They found an eddy in the crowd, claimed their space, and began.

She was looser now, so her shimmy slid easily into full sway. The heat ate from her hips into her arms and legs. She sped up the tempo. He stayed with her. The man knew his body. He knew how to dance.

Lisa leaned closer, matching her moves to his. Close enough to feel his warmth without touching him. The air between them flared. Her movement went molten. The drum was her heart, her limbs were the strings, and her blood surged beyond her skin. This was it. This was what she'd come for.

To be the music. To be in her body. The music let her in, into her scary, tender body. She held it as long as she could, and his body held for her, and the music held them both.

The song ended and she fell back, as if swooning a little, settling into a hand's more space between them.

"Thank you so much for the dance, that was wonderful," she breathed into Mark's ear, barely brushing her breast against his shirt. She pressed her fingers into his hand. "Let's do it again sometime." She turned away. She could go home now, and be satisfied.

"Would you like a drink?" he asked.

She turned and looked him over again. If she did this, how long would he be good for? How long if she did not? He withstood her gaze, his eyes hot and unwavering. The flames shot her through again, the power and the song. She let the heat show on her face. They broke into simultaneous smiles. "I think I would like that," Lisa said.

They returned to the bar, the hand on her back giving her chills.

She sipped her wine while her body burned with hot and cold, pleasure and panic. She wanted to pull him to the floor for more. She didn't remember what she said. She forgot to school her eyes, to prevent what they might promise. Then he asked her to dance again. He touched her again. And did not release her when they made it to the floor, but lifted her hand in his.

They swept into an easy swing step, their bodies coming a mere breath apart, and then falling back, pendulums marking the heated core, never closing completely but never letting go. Over and over until Lisa felt it impossible that the next heartbeat did not bring Mark's lips crashing down onto hers. But he obeyed the steps of the dance. They obeyed, the two as one. It was beyond perfection.

When it was over, she drew back, flushed to her depths. She looked down; her bosom was visibly heaving, just like the romance novels said. His eyes followed hers. He stepped closer. His arms encircled her. Too close! She wanted to run, or maybe she wanted to hike her skirt and have him take her here and now. But she laid her head gently on his shoulder. His arms tightened. The dance continued, oh so very softly now. Lisa made a mental note to tip the DJ for putting on a ballad next.

Gently moving, swaying closer, inch by luxurious inch, more and more of Mark and Lisa touched. Her arms slowly snaked, her breasts pressed, her thighs rubbed. He stroked her hair. His breath tickled her bent neck. They did not miss a step.

The song ended. They stopped. They did not move apart but stood as if turned to stone. The crowd, the music, moved on around them. She couldn't bear for this to end, for life to stop being less than this moment. This was the time of her life.

But it stopped; of course it stopped. Mark inclined his head and kissed her neck and she shivered in his arms. She pulled away.

She led him off the dance floor; he followed eagerly. But she made her excuses. Leaving him sure that she was too refined a girl to sleep with him so soon, but that if she stayed in his presence any longer she didn't know what she might do, he was that sexy. Tomorrow night, she promised. She'd be back to dance tomorrow night.

He insisted on walking her to her car. She took his arm. He took her keys and unlocked her door. And then he did kiss her lips, and it felt fine, but nowhere near so fine as his hand on her back on the dance floor.

Copacabana

It was too fragrant an April evening to be stuck behind a sour beery bar. Through the opened French doors of Promises, Wendy gazed at what she could see of budding branches against the deepening sky. She thought of watercolors, the pigments dissolving beneath her wet brush to release their sweetest hues. She gazed and caught with her peripheral vision when she should nod or smile or pour another drink for the men gazing at her. Her body served them and didn't shy from their eyes. Their tips bought her brushes.

The guys were regulars, quiet men who left when the sky grew dark and the disco music started. A couple loan officers from the bank down the street — they ordered the bottled beer rather than the cheaper draft, liking to watch her bend down into the cooler to fetch it. An older medical supply salesman, who lived around the corner and had been drinking in this spot long before its latest incarnation, drank his martinis straight up. Shaken, not stirred. She did make a great dry martini. A bit of vermouth in the glass, swirl it around and pour it right out — that was the trick. She shook the gin with ice, and the men watched her breasts jiggle. She looked at her watch as she strained and poured the chilled liquor. Just a couple more hours to go.

She'd work on her latest piece when she got home. A study in chalk pastels on black paper of Marie Laveau's littered tomb. The dead Voodoo queen still received offerings of fruit and flowers from folks who believed she could grant them their heart's desire. She'd been inspired by her recent visit to the old St. Louis cemetery, the avenues of tiny temples, a city of the eternal dead among the decay of the living.

Wendy's attention snapped with a start when she saw her grandmother walk in the door.

No, thank goodness, not her grandmother, but another sweet, white haired lady in a light blue dress. She'd hate for Gram to see her dressed like this. Wendy tugged up on the tube top that mostly covered her breasts. With a chest like hers, "mostly" still exposed an interesting amount.

The elderly lady carefully walked the length of the bar and sat on a stool at the far end.

"Who's that, you think?" Wendy asked her little group. The two younger men shrugged. The salesman mumbled, "She comes around now and then" and became more interested in his drink.

Wendy walked over to the woman and smiled. "What can I get for you today?" The woman flicked her eyes in Wendy's direction. "Whiskey sour, please."

Wendy scooped up ice in a highball glass. With one hand she poured out bourbon, with another the sour mix, then added the orange slice and cherry garnish. "Whiskey sour," Wendy said cheerfully, spinning a napkin out from a stack and setting the drink in front of the woman.

The older woman picked a couple bills carefully out of a coin purse and set them down. Her eyes looked somewhere Wendy couldn't find. Wendy went back to the men who'd been following her with theirs.

But Wendy didn't go back to looking at the sky. She watched the old woman sip her drink. Wendy named her Lola, after the showgirl trapped in time in that Barry Manilow song. Had this woman had a tragic past? Had she also left a part her mind somewhere, somewhere she thought was better than now? Wendy smiled at herself.

Maybe Lola just wanted a drink, and to hell with what other people thought.

Wendy would do her portrait in batik, she thought. It was a new medium she'd wanted to try. She imagined the layers of Lola's face as the work progressed, her youth disappearing beneath the cracked web of age.

Lola had another drink, closed her eyes, and swayed on the barstool. Wendy's heart shot to her throat. If she should fall! But the woman lifted her hands, almost like a conductor. Lola was dancing. Wendy wondered with whom.

She lost track of the woman as evening became night. The early guys left, to be replaced by men staking a claim to a barstool for the night. Some couples arrived, having a drink before going elsewhere. Wendy stopped seeing color and composition. She saw signaling hands and empty glasses. By the next lull, Lola was gone and the French doors had been shut against the sky.

Toni, the cocktail waitress, was on duty. "Two Cuba Libres" was her way of saying hello. She'd chat plenty to the guys with cash, but Wendy wasn't worth that much of her time. Wendy squeezed lime into rum and coke and thought, Toni was like Lola, she lived in her own world too. And didn't Wendy?

She ran from one end of the bar to the other, scooping, pouring, ringing up cash, and tugging up her top when it slipped low. Where the hell was Tommy? It was past time for him to relieve her. Was it the full moon? Something in the air promised a wild night, and people drank hard in preparation.

Tommy sauntered in. He stopped to chat with his buddy, Mike, the bar owner, also recently arrived.

Wendy narrowed a glare in their direction, then plastered her automatic smile back on. Her handful of quiet lonely men, easily managed, had become a hungry horde.

"I've got money. I've got drugs. Give me sex!" Some guys might as well be shouting it out loud. It gave her a headache.

When Tommy did step behind the bar, he did it in full swing, talking with four people at once, his hands filling glasses with ice and booze as if they had eyes of their own. He never looked around when he pulled out bottles of the expensive liquor behind him. He knew exactly where everything was. His arms were like propellers. Wendy ducked into the cubby to count out the take from her shift and to get her purse.

When she came out, Tommy had a drink waiting for her—a strawberry daiquiri, one of the fancy frozen kinds not included in the usual freebies allowed to bartenders. She loved strawberries. He winked at her, and Wendy had to smile back. He was a devil, but he was a cute one. Better to laugh than be mad with guys like him. Besides she was free now, for the entire weekend. She felt generous.

She took the drink, but she didn't want to watch Tommy flirt and pour. She rarely stayed around after work; she didn't know where she belonged if not behind the bar. Certainly not in the back with the cozy couples. She hadn't gotten close to anyone. She was just passing through this town. Making money to keep heading west, to see the world, and make her art along the way.

But art was keeping her here, so far for a month longer than her original plan. New Orleans was so thick; Wendy hadn't begun to see and touch and smell it all. She suddenly realized her plans for her cross-country adventure had become vague without her knowing. Without them, she felt even more alone.

There was nowhere she belonged.

She sipped her drink, and the rum, sugar and ice rushed to her head. In the midst of brain-freeze, Wendy flashed on a batik of herself, seeing the frost of age creep over her own fresh face. But she'd never be like Lola. She'd get married and have kids, some day. Not drink by herself in a bar and go home with a salesman when she felt emptier than usual.

Like tonight. The freeze faded, but not the sudden desperation. It left her hollow. She was lonelier than she wanted to admit. She hadn't had anyone to love since she'd left Jake in Florida. She ached, not for him, but for the memory. She should find someone. Someone nice, decent. She didn't have to be alone all the time. And it didn't have to be forever.

She sipped again, and wandered towards the front of the bar. The rum zinged in her blood. She didn't drink much hard liquor, and Tommy made a strong drink.

Someone nice. Not like Mike, she added vehemently, as the bar owner leered at her chest and at the daiquiri in her hand.

"Hey, Wendy, having a drink?" Mike said, without looking up at her face.

"Yes, thanks so much!" Wendy tipped her glass, shot him her most saccharin smile, and kept walking.

She was almost to the front door.

"Have a seat?" Steve the doorman to the rescue. He had a bar stool behind his podium, but often preferred to stand.

"Thanks, Steve." Wendy sat, while he stood near, looking over the incoming crowd. She relaxed in the relative quiet of her corner, sipped her drink, and watched Steve do his job.

He looked good for an older guy. Rugged. Toni had said he was already thirty. And that he worked as a carpenter during the day. Toni knew all the gossip.

"Sorry, man. The rules are you've got to be twenty-one," Steve said to a group of freshmen frat boys.

"Where are you from, man? The drinking age is still eighteen in this state!"

"But not in this club. Sorry. Here, let me get the door for you."

Steve smoothly shut them out, turned, and caught Wendy's smile. She liked the way he handled them.

"You know I'm not twenty-one until July," she said, raising her voice above the general din.

"But the rules don't apply to girls like you," he said, grinning. And he didn't glance down from her eyes while he said it.

He came back to stand by her. She felt his warmth. "Are you from around here?" she asked.

"No, Chicago. It was too cold up there for me. And you?"

"Florida. The part where there's nothing but orange groves."

"Sounds like we've both come a long way."

"Yes."

They fell into peaceful silence. Steve watched the door; Wendy sipped her drink. The music and the chatter washed over and around them, but they were undisturbed. As if together they made their own quiet place.

Lisa, a regular night customer, walked in and waved to them. "She's dressed to kill tonight," Wendy murmured.

"I've never seen her leave with anyone though. The guys who walk her out come right back in," Steve said.

"Funny, I thought getting a man would be the whole point of coming here dressed like that." Wendy looked down at her own skimpy outfit. She blushed. They both laughed a little. Steve's eyes crinkled in the nicest way. She studied his face.

"You notice most everything, don't you, Steve?"

He leaned in to speak softly in her ear.

"I've noticed you, Wendy. You never leave with anyone either. You're just here to work. Like I am."

"Something else we have in common."

"Yes." His breath prickled her skin. His eyes looked down into hers. But he pulled back abruptly. "Whoa, there!" He stopped a couple on their way out the door. "Let me get you some plastic cups for those."

The man protested. "We're going to be right outside, we're not leaving." But Steve had already pulled the glass from his hand and poured its contents into a cup he got from a stack on the podium. His date handed hers over without another word. "Thanks, guys," Steve said. He set the glasses into a dish tub behind him and turned back to Wendy.

She had finished her drink. She set her glass in the tub too. She couldn't sit here watching him work all night. That would be pathetic. She may be lonely and now a little loopy, but it was time she left. "Thank you for the seat, Steve, and for the company."

"Wendy, wait." Steve took a deep breath. She watched his shirt stretch across his chest. "Would you go out with me tomorrow?"

If he wants to meet me at a bar, forget it! Wendy thought, startled, though she automatically smiled.

"I thought we could have a picnic lunch in Audubon Park. It's beautiful this time of year. Say about one o' clock?"

He looked earnest. And strong. And she loved the park. Wendy's smile deepened beyond her pretty face. "That sounds nice," she said. "I'll meet you near the entrance." Then she could leave when she wanted.

"Can I bring anything?" she added politely.

"Not a thing." *He really did have nice eyes,* she thought, *and a good smile.* "I'll see you then, Wendy." He pressed her fingers lightly. Her heart jumped. Damn rum.

"I'll look forward to it."

He held the door, and she stepped outside. The night was fresh and clear. The air was soft as a kiss.

Wendy drove home to her apartment, her smile staying with her. And she realized her words to Steve were true. She was looking forward, to something besides the next town along Interstate Ten, the next place to say she'd been.

Got To Be Real

So here goes, Wendy thought, *my first date in months*. She shouldn't feel nervous. She'd been out with plenty of guys, and had been in love with a few. She wasn't nursing some secret heartache. And Steve was just a guy, a nice guy who built houses and watched over clubs on weekends for a few extra bucks. But it had been a while. She'd shut off that side of herself when she hit the road.

There was another thing. Last night, after working for hours on Marie Laveau's chalk drawing, she'd dreamt about him. She couldn't remember what it was that left her with a pang in her heart when she woke up. As if something about this day would change her life forever.

He stood near the entrance of the park, carrying an enormous basket and wearing a grin to match. From the front, Audubon Park looked nice but ordinary, a large suburban lawn dotted with trees and regiments of flowers. But the drives and walks wound through arches of overhanging oak hung with moss, giving eerie shadows on the brightest of days. Paths led to cozy glades next to a musical creek.

"Let's find a nice spot, shall we?" Steve said.

They wandered; they talked little. Wendy stared up at the ancient trees. The oaks lined Saint Charles Avenue too, but here she could get closer without trespassing, and walk right beneath them, and touch them. Their skin was rough. Their veils were tattered. Somber and romantic, much like her mood.

"They're wonderful, aren't they? So mysterious," said Steve. "I never get tired of coming here."

17

Wendy stared at him wonder. Steve's words, dovetailing with her thoughts, wrapped around her like a spell.

They found a place beneath one of the weeping trees. Steve spread out the blanket and unpacked the basket. Wendy unpacked her own bag, bringing out her sketchpad and drawing pencils. *Love me, love my art*, she thought when she decided to bring them. She wasn't going to lose a day of springtime for anyone. But now her hands shook strangely as she began to sketch the scene.

Steve opened and poured champagne for them both. He didn't make small talk, but seemed content to watch her draw. "I like that," he said, when she set her pencil down.

He brought so much food! Fried chicken and coleslaw, fluffy rolls, strawberries and cream.

"Wow!" said Wendy, helping herself. "Mmmm, delicious, too." The food settled her down, returning her to the realm of the ordinary. Her hands weren't shaking anymore. What was she so worried about?

"Thank you," said Steve. "I like to cook."

"You made all this yourself?"

"I was inspired." He smiled at her. "Do you like to cook?"

"I haven't done much of it. I used to like baking cookies with my grandma."

"Maybe you'd like to learn."

"Maybe I would." Wendy smiled back at Steve. But she wouldn't ask for lessons, not yet.

She finished eating and sighed in satisfaction. She stretched out on the blanket and rolled over on her stomach. She picked up her sketchbook and gestured towards Steve. "Do you mind?" she asked.

"Not at all," he said. He lay back on the blanket beside her and looked up at the sky. She looked at him.

It was true his face was more fallen, more settled, and rougher in texture than the other guys she'd dated. But the eyes were kinder, wiser eyes. She'd never sketched someone so close up. When her pencil outlined his cheekbone it almost felt like her finger was tracing the line on his skin. She completed his face and her pencil stopped, but her eyes moved on down to his chest and arms. In his T-shirt it was obvious he worked with his body for a living.

"Do you like being a carpenter? What do you like to build most?" she asked.

"I like making furniture. I've made most of my own. Someday I'd like to build my own house."

Wendy's heart skipped. "I used to dream about having a house in the woods, where everything in it would be handmade to my design, from the shape of the windows to the pattern on the dishes."

"I'd like to live in the country too," Steve said. "But the work is here."

"Well, here is pretty nice for now," Wendy said, smiling, high on wine and springtime. The tulips flung their colors at her shamelessly.

Steve raised himself on one elbow and turned to face her. "Here is absolutely perfect now." He reached out and brushed back a strand of hair from her face.

Wendy shivered. She couldn't stop herself. She looked away. He dropped his hand. He gazed at her, sober and serious. He wanted. But he wouldn't push.

Wendy lay on her back, and gazed up at the tree. Steve lay beside her. Not touching, yet she felt him from head to toe. She felt all she'd been missing in her life on the road. In her restless nights, when she stayed up for hours painting, and not always because she was inspired. She missed having someone solid and real around. And here was a man who'd matured beyond leering and copping a feel. A man who could mold the dark heart of wood with his hands.

She turned to him and he to her.

He cupped her cheek in his palm. She could feel the calluses. Her eyes lowered and her lips parted. Kiss me, they whispered.

His lips were warm and firm, and turned hers soft and hot. She brought her hand to the back of his neck. Press harder, her hand said. Go deeper. Steve's mouth obeyed.

Children shrieked and a ball bounced near their heads. They broke apart and sat up. "Sorry! We're sorry!" the children shouted. They retrieved their ball, and ran off.

Wendy laughed, near breathless. "Aren't they cute?" she managed to say.

Steve handed Wendy a full champagne glass. "Let's have a toast," he said.

"To?"

"To finding something so real in the most unreal of places."

"Oh," she breathed. Wendy's heart grew fluttering wings. "I'll drink to that."

They drained their glasses. They tossed them aside. She reached out with both arms and pulled him down to her. She needed his weight to keep her here on earth. She needed another kiss to keep her from flying above it. A kiss that was sweet and strong and endless.

She got what she wanted. The kiss did last forever. Because when it ended, everything had changed. Steve had to go get ready for work, and Wendy was in love.

"I hate to leave you." Steve helped Wendy stand up. "I want us to be able to spend time together, without any interruption."

"I want that too."

"Tomorrow's Sunday, and I'm not working. Are you?"

"No."

"Oh, damn! I just remembered I told a friend I'd help him move. And we're both working all next week... How about Sunday next? I'll pick you up at ten and we'll have the whole day."

"All right." But Wendy was not all right. Sunday next?! To wait more than a week before kissing him again? How could he want to wait so long?

Steve smiled and touched her lips gently with his forefinger. "It's a date then." He kissed her again. Just for a moment, but it was full of promise. Wendy's tremulous smile turned radiant.

"Come on. Let me take you back to your car."

Wendy did not remember the walk back. She was freezing and burning and swirling, a fancy drink in a blender. She was amazed that she could walk at all. That they found her car. She watched as her hand scribbled down her phone number and address.

He held her close one last time. "Until then," he whispered.

"Until then." She promised him back.

Ladies Night

"Hey, Wendy! Can we get a backgammon board? And two white wines, please." Some guy at the bar tossed Lisa heavy glances, but she didn't play catch. She wasn't here to dance tonight. It was Ladies Night. She was here to be with her best friend.

The theory behind Ladies Night was that women would flock to bars for the free drinks. The men were pumped to swoop down on them when they showed. But like any other night, the men outnumbered the women. For Lisa and Claire, Ladies Night meant time to spend together, without having to get men to buy drinks for them.

"But sugar," Claire would say, "men paying for us is only fair. They don't spend nearly what we do on their hair and faces and clothes. And we do all that for them."

The girls sat down, opened the board, and each rolled a die. Claire rolled a three, Lisa a one. Claire made her five point. A good start for her game. Not so good for Lisa's. But it was early; anything could happen.

Lisa pointed with her chin towards the door. "That's Mark," she said.

"The great dancer?"

"Yeah."

"He's cute!"

"Yeah, he is." Lisa smiled, happy that Claire approved.

Mark sauntered up to their table. "Hello, ladies."

"Hi, Mark. This is my friend, Claire."

"Hi, Mark."

"Claire," he nodded. Mark paused a fraction of a second. Then he lowered his voice and turned to Lisa with an intimate smile. "So. How about a dance, lovely?"

"I'm sorry. We're playing a game just now."

"And I'm winning so far." Claire picked up her cup and shook her dice.

Mark's eyebrows drew together. "Later then?"

"Later." Lisa smiled up at him, willing him to understand and to go away. He went away.

"He doesn't look happy," Claire said.

Lisa shrugged. "What can I do? Guys always think they're more important than anything else."

"I thought you liked him."

"I do! But I like you more."

They watched Mark approach another girl. He glanced back at Lisa to see if she noticed.

Lisa sighed. "Well. That may be it."

"Lisa. Don't you get lonely?"

Lisa stared at her friend.

One side of Claire's face was pulled into the smallest of smiles.

"I mean, don't you get horny?"

Lisa laughed. "Oh, shut up and roll. But speaking of, what's with you and Charlie?" Lisa tried to sound like she cared.

Claire's polished nail twisted in her feathered hair. "He's history. He stood me up once too often."

Lisa suppressed a cheer, grateful now for Claire's busy schedule at the hotel. Anyone in management was expected to put in hours of unpaid overtime. Claire's free time was precious, and wasting it waiting on a man wouldn't sit well with her.

"He sure was hot, though." It was Claire's turn to sigh.

"If you say so. You know I never could see the attraction." Charlie was Claire's ideal physical type, that was the trouble. Tall, blond, and tanned, with glacial blue eyes. Like a Northern god. Lisa preferred someone warmer.

"Did I tell you about the last time with him? He tied my hands to the bedposts!" Claire paused for effect. Lisa tried to not to show her shock. In stories, nasty men sometimes did that to the heroines. She'd known Charlie was a sleaze from the start.

"It was the wildest time I've ever had. I loved it—him thinking he was so in control, but doing all he could to please me and make me crazy."

"I don't think I'd like that much," said Lisa. Actually, she knew she'd hate it, being at the mercy of some guy. She shuddered. Sometimes she didn't understand Claire at all.

Lisa was no virgin, so it wasn't like she was a prude. Her old boyfriend back home had begged and begged, and said it would prove their love. She'd been curious, having read and heard so much about it. But doing it hadn't proved anything. He still begged, and she remained unsatisfied.

Dancing was better. Being Claire's friend and hearing about her adventures was better. Claire was looking at her now, arching one eyebrow in that way she had. Time to change the subject.

"So, should we find you somebody new?" Lisa said.

Claire smiled like a cat. "Maybe I'll take a break," she said.

Lisa somehow doubted it.

Toni stopped by the table. "Can I get you ladies a refill?" Toni let most of the ladies get their own free drinks, but unlike others, Claire and Lisa would tip a dollar a drink for the service.

"Yes, please," Claire said. "What happened to Karen?"

"Oh, she got a job tending bar at some barbecue place downtown," said Toni. "Just pouring beer, really, but good tips. Plus she got mad at Mike and 'fell in love' with this new owner." Toni shifted a hip and pouted. "I've got too many shifts. And I've got finals coming up. You know anyone who needs a job?"

Lisa did. "My neighbor, Jess. I'll let her know."

Toni went to get the drinks. Lisa turned to Claire. "That'd be fun to have Jess here. Remember I told you about her. I'm sure she'd like this place better than that smelly diner."

"SNAKE EYES!" Loud enough to penetrate the general din, the shout from the next table made both women jump.

It was the gamblers. Men intent on a backgammon board, sitting and playing, or gathered around waiting to play, winning or losing hundreds of dollars a night. They weren't looking for women, not yet, anyway. Business came first.

The shout came from Eddie. Fast Eddie, they called him. Everybody knew him. His booming voice, his lucky yellow shirt, and his occasional burst of generosity. Just last week he'd bought a round for everyone in the bar.

"Just what I needed! Now doesn't that beat all!"

His opponent glowered at the outburst and at the dice Eddie had rolled. But he didn't look up at Eddie, who'd leapt out of his chair to clap the other fellows on the back to celebrate his good luck. The other player studied the board instead. In seconds it seemed like a dozen calculations spun in his dark gaze.

Toni was back at the women's table with the white wine. "Who's that playing Eddie?" Claire asked her. "I know I've seen him around."

"His name is Jackson. He's from around here." 'Here' meant he was an uptown boy, from one private-school girl to another. "Remember the teen club that Sacred Heart sponsored? He used to hang out there sometimes. He went to the boy's school."

"He doesn't seem like the other boys."

"Oh, he thinks he's too smart for everyone else. He never tips more than a quarter for his beer, since that's the closest he can get to an exact fifteen percent."

Lisa felt left out. Even if Claire said Toni was a gold digger and a slut, a common background connected them, and Lisa could never be part of that. Oh, how she wished she'd lived here all her life! Then she might share those looks. Lisa looked over Claire's new object of interest, trying to figure out the attraction this time. A different type of guy, Jackson had black springy hair, moonlit skin, and hooded eyes.

Toni moved on to another customer, and the players continued their game. Jackson handled his pips with precise white fingers. But he had a body that she was sure didn't know how to dance. Lisa was baffled.

"He looks interesting," Claire said. "Intense."

"He doesn't smile."

Claire shrugged an elegant shoulder. "We'll see about that."

This guy wouldn't last either, Lisa reminded herself. Aloud she said, "It's your turn."

Claire shook and spilled the dice. Double ones. "Snake eyes," she said.

Lisa watched Claire watch Jackson. The strength of Claire's gaze slowly forced his eyes up from the board. It was incredible. She was like a sorceress summoning a demon. Claire chose, and the man came to her. Lisa only knew how to set a lure and wait, and then hope she liked what she attracted. Claire was amazing.

Claire gave Jackson a long slow smile.

After a stare of two heartbeats, he nodded his head, saluting her. He turned back to the board. His concentration was broken, but it appeared fortune turned his way, for he won the game after a few more minutes. But instead of taking on the next comer, Jackson abdicated his position, picked up his winnings and stalked to the bar.

He watched Claire now, from behind her back. Lisa kept half an eye on him. Claire took no notice, and continued chatting about people they both knew. But Lisa knew better.

Claire finished her wine. She got up. "I'm going to get another," she said. "Want one too?"

Lisa shook her head. Though Claire would come back eventually, just like the gambler would return to his game, she wasn't going to hold her breath. Lisa looked around, and saw Mark. He was talking to another girl, but looking at her. She wondered how long he'd been looking. He didn't have the snake eyes, that was for sure.

But he did have a body made to dance. Lisa smiled, and stood up. Mark was by her side in a few short steps. Then he was escorting her to the floor.

Lisa's body moved with his, but her mind floated above. *He doesn't know me,* she thought. *I don't even know his last name.*

But talking didn't matter. What mattered was this, the bodily rapport. That meant everything. Not talking, not thinking, but feeling. Dancing.

The song ended, and Mark stopped. He led Lisa to a Victorian love seat in the back. Lisa waited, her heart pounding, her eyes cast down. She knew it was time for this. Mark would not dance with her forever; guys weren't like that. They wanted more. Lisa... maybe she wanted more too. But she didn't know how to make it happen.

How she could be more like Claire? She couldn't see Claire anymore, but she imagined her, enchanting Jackson with her eyes and her curving lips, with a touch on his slim white hand.

Lisa looked up. Mark's face was closer than she expected. She lifted her hand and caressed his cheek. Soft above, rough below. He caught her fingers and brought them to his lips. His lips were soft, but too moist. When he let them go to kiss her lips, she didn't wipe them on her skirt, that wouldn't be romantic, but she gripped his shirt to surreptitiously dry them there. He pressed his mouth harder to hers. And that wasn't what she wanted, but she guessed it was what she'd asked for. She sighed. He plundered on. It was awful.

Mark lifted his head. His eyes burned with lust, hers with unshed tears. She pushed him away. "I'm sorry. I have to go." She stood. He looked angry and confused and she didn't blame him. But she couldn't explain. She didn't know him enough to know where to begin. "I'm sorry," she said again. She rushed away.

Claire sat like a pirate queen in the circle of gamblers, directing their fortunes with her smiles. Lisa strode up to her. "I think I'll head home now. See you tomorrow?"

"Sure thing, sugar," Claire replied. She frowned at Lisa's flushed face, but didn't ask. She trusted Lisa to know her own business. Funny, when Lisa didn't trust herself.

Tonight's The Night

In the late morning light, with its chipped mirrors and cheesy, flocked wallpaper, Promises didn't look much like the place Lisa had described. But it was still a sight better than the burger joint. A beefy man hunched over some papers at the bar, holding his head in his hands. Jess cleared her throat and he glanced up.

"Are you Mike?" she asked.

"Yeah," he grunted. "What do you want?"

"The waitress job."

"Come closer."

She handed him her resume, skimpy as it was. He stared blankly at the piece of paper, tossed it aside, and looked her up and down.

"You ever waitress before?"

"Yes, at Duff's Diner..." Her voice trailed off. It was on the resume, and he wasn't listening.

"Well, the others who came in were dogs, so you'll do. Start tonight at seven. Toni will show you what to do." Mike looked back at his order forms, dismissing her.

He's a real charmer, Jess thought. *But the tips in this place should bring her income to a whole new level. Her old car was on its last legs; she could use the money.*

Start work tonight! Just like that, on a Friday night. Sink or swim time. Well, she'd never been afraid of a challenge. Her papa used to say the only way to get her to do something was to tell her she couldn't.

Back at her apartment, she called home to tell them the news.

"You know I'm happy if you're happy, Jessalyn," her mama said. "But there's bad girls working in places like that. You've always been a little wild, but you're a good girl at heart. Don't you let that place mess you up!"

"Oh Mama, don't worry. Nothing will happen to me." Jess couldn't imagine what Mama was worried about. Serving a drink or serving a meal were pretty much the same.

What was she going to wear? In Bayou Teche her sexiest clothes were cutoffs and halter tops. Her two dressy outfits had family event written all over them. She had to go shopping! It would eat into her savings, but Jess was sure the investment would pay off. This was the beginning of a new life in the big city, and it was going to be great.

At seven o'clock, Jess had a red dress on, a sultry slip of one. It blazed, and her sun-bronzed skin soaked up the heat. She felt radiant with power and promise.

The place looked good in the evening light. No more grease smell! And music! She danced as she walked the length of the bar.

"Hi! You must be Toni. I'm Jess."

Toni looked her up and down. How weird that it reminded her so much of Mike's stare.

"Write your name on the top of this time card. There's where you punch in. Here's the drink trays. Get a glass from the bartender to keep your money in. Always put down a napkin first. You serve the tables in the back and I take the front."

No one was sitting in the back yet. Jess raised an eyebrow. "You can watch me for a while," said Toni.

Wendy came over to the two women. "That's Wendy," Toni continued. "The daytime bartender. She'll be gone soon as Tommy gets here for the night shift."

Jess raised both eyebrows at that. What a rude girl! Her mama didn't have to worry about Jess becoming like that. She was raised better. Wendy shook her head and smiled at Jess. "Welcome to Promises," Wendy said. "And don't mind her."

Toni pretended she didn't hear that. She walked off to serve a new arrival, and Jess watched. The guy hadn't sat down, but there was Toni, asking what he wanted. He might walk to the bar and order himself, but if she got there first, the tip would be hers.

The work was simple enough, much like waiting tables. Jess paid attention to how Toni listed the drinks she ordered from Wendy. First came the frozen drinks so they could get started in the blender, then house liquor drinks (in scotch, bourbon, gin, vodka, rum, tequila order, just as the bottles were lined up in the well), then call liquor, then beer and wine. Finally a few couples arrived and sat in the back, and Jess was on her own.

Drink trays were smaller than food trays, and balancing a full one was no problem for Jess. Remembering the prices was harder. But Wendy kept up a running commentary to help her out. "Well drinks are two dollars, and call liquor three. One scotch and water and one Seven and Seven is five."

"Thanks, Wendy. You're the best."

"No problem," she said. "We've all had a first day."

Around nine, Wendy signaled Jess. "This is Tommy. Tommy, this is Jess. She's a good girl, so be nice." She turned to Jess. "I'll see you next week. I'm sure you'll do great. Bye y'all."

"Bye, Wendy," Jess said, but she was still looking at Tommy. He was gorgeous! He smiled at her and said, "So, darlin', are you a good girl?"

Jess grinned back. "Very good," she said. And wouldn't she just like to show him! His green eyes were to die for!

Tommy laughed and said, "I think I like you." Then he turned to a young woman leaning over and pushing her breasts up against the bar. "Well now, what can I do for you tonight, darlin'?"

So Tommy was a flirt. Jess shrugged. It came with the job. She knew from the diner how the right smile at the right time turned a fifty-cent tip into a buck.

Jess did her job. She smiled and served drinks and collected money in a growing whirlwind of bodies and sound.

"Whew!" she exclaimed, as she ordered yet another round for a large and boisterous group. "Don't these people ever let up?"

"People drink real fast in the beginning," Tommy told her. "They'll slow down after they start feeling it more."

Probably after the couples began making out more too, rather than merely flirting. Several of them looked headed in that direction.

On her next trip to the bar, she ran into Lisa.

"Jess! It's great to see you here," Lisa said. "How do you like it so far?"

"I think I like it!" Jess laughed. "But I'll have to let you know when my head stops spinning!"

When the pace finally relented, Jess checked her watch. It was two o'clock in the morning. Lisa and the biggest press of the crowd were gone. The couples in the back were as good as gone too, lost in lust as they were. Jess stood at the waitress station sipping a Coke. Mike and a buddy of his were drinking at the bar.

"There's the new girl." Mike pointed at Jess.

"She's a looker," the buddy said. "Hey, new girl! Come over here. I've got a big tip for you." He patted his lap and the two guys cracked up.

"Yeah, new girl. Come over here," said Mike.

"No, thanks," Jess replied. "I'm just fine where I am."

Mike scowled. Tommy stepped out from behind the bar to stand at Jess's side. He put his arm around her shoulders, looked down at her possessively, and drawled, "Yeah, Mike, she's just fine where she is."

"Ha ha!" the buddy said. "He beat you to her."

Mike's scowl darkened. Toni slid up between Mike and his friend. They both put their free, non-drinking hands on her. "I go for big tips, don't I, Mike? Now what can I get for you big boys?"

The buddy's drink was full, but he fished a ten out of his pocket. "Get me some cigarettes, sweetheart."

Mike sneered at Jess. He also gave Toni a ten. "Get me some too."

Cigarettes were two dollars from the machine. Toni gloated at Jess on her way to buy them. "I just made sixteen bucks."

"And I'm just thrilled for you," Jess retorted sweetly. Tommy laughed.

Now there was a bad girl, Jess thought. Someone who would suck up to creeps for sixteen dollars. She hoped she'd never get that desperate. She did a quick count of her tips so far. It was more than she made in three nights at the diner. More than enough to keep her self-respect. She picked up her tray and made another round of her tables.

In another hour, most of her tables had cleared. Mike told her to punch out and check the schedule he posted by the time clock. She did, and then asked Tommy for her purse that Wendy had stashed behind the bar.

He handed it to her and said, "Hey, Jess, how about having a drink and keeping me company?"

He didn't call her "darlin'" like he had been all night. He called her by her name. She liked that. "I'll have a beer."

"Ah, a girl after my own heart," said Tommy. He poured two drafts, one for her and one for himself. They clicked glasses. "Here's to your first day done."

"And to you for helping me through it," Jess said earnestly. "Really. Thank you." She touched his hand like she would touch a friend.

Tommy's smooth surface rippled the tiniest bit. Then the patented smile grew wider. "Why, you make it real easy, darlin'. I'll help you through any old night you need."

I Feel Love

Wendy wore a lacy low cut summer dress. Steve's face flamed when he saw her. "You look terrific," he said. Wendy, wanting to throw herself into his arms and unable to think of anything else, managed for the moment to look demure.

Steve took her arm and led her to his car. He opened the door for her. He was a perfect gentleman. Just perfect, she sighed, as he touched her, helping her in. Too perfect, she sighed, since he hadn't ravaged her on sight.

He took her to the French Market. They walked hand in hand among stalls selling okra and alligator tail, T-shirts and religious figurines. Vendors rapped about their wares. Buyers muttered their prevarications. Their noise swarmed around and between Wendy and Steve. She took his arm and pressed against his side. But he was still too far away. She needed him closer than her skin.

"I want to get some hot sauce. This place makes the best. Have you tried it? Do you like pralines? We can pick some up if you like." Steve talked and Wendy nodded and murmured. And worried. Didn't he want to kiss her? Didn't he remember? She'd thought of nothing else since.

Finally he finished his shopping. He steered her away from the market toward a nearby restaurant. In the booth, he slid in beside her. She twisted her torso to face him. She stared and flushed, feeling alone and shameful in her desire.

The waitress brought the menus. He ordered drinks and appetizers for them and sent her away.

Steve turned, and took Wendy's hand in his. He looked into her eyes. In that look was all Wendy wanted, all she could ever want. It looked like love to her.

The waitress brought the drinks. They reached out as one and tipped their glasses to each other. They sipped together the sweet, sharp liquor.

Need swelled and broke over her. She could not sit and play at being civilized one more minute. She pulled Steve's head to her and drove her mouth against his. She swept her outer leg up and between his. Her knee grazed his lap.

"Wendy!" Steve gasped. He straightened up and looked around.

She drew back a little. "I had to know." Her voice rasped. "I had to know if you still wanted me."

"Want you?! I'm crazy for you! You are the most amazing girl I've ever met!"

Wendy beamed and leaned forward to kiss him again.

Steve held her back, his hands on her shoulders.

"Don't!" whispered Wendy. "Don't hold me back. And don't hold back from me."

Steve's face was serious. "If you don't want me to hold back, then we need to get out of here right now."

"Then let's get out of here right now." Her fingertips trailed down his neck.

"But the food..."

"I don't want the food." She touched his lips. She licked hers. He raised his hands in surrender.

"All right. Though you might want it later," he said teasingly. Wendy laughed, her face alight.

He threw some money down and they tumbled out of the restaurant. When he would reach across her to open her car door, she turned, and she was in his arms.

She wrapped her arms around his back. She gave her weight to the car behind her, and wrapped her legs around him too. She made him kiss her again, soft but deep.

Her legs. Her smooth long legs. His hands could not help but stroke them, and then her strong thighs, pushing her skirt up towards her hips.

She opened her legs wider. Until she felt it. The hardness in his jeans, against the thinnest layer of her silken panties, with her soft and damp beneath.

The kiss became a flow of fire, from mouth to crotch, from him to her and back again.

Steve broke away with a moan. "God, Wendy. I have got to get you home." He opened the car door, and she sank into her seat.

Neither of them spoke on the ride to his place.

On the walk to his door.

As he opened the door.

Then he was lifting her, carrying her, crushing her to his chest, and that he could do this when she was not a petite girl made Wendy love him all the more. She listened to his beating heart and felt that there was nothing she would not do for this man.

He set her down on his rough-hewn four-poster bed. He stood over her and she looked up at him, too far away. She reached out her arms to pull him down to her. He ignored them and stared fiercely into her eyes. Wendy dropped her arms. He wants me, she told herself, but he needs to be the one in charge. He unbuttoned his shirt, still staring down at her. He slipped off his shoes, and Wendy did the same.

She scooted back and away, making room on the bed for him. Retreating so he must come after her and capture her again. He did. He came to her. He pinned her body under his. She closed her eyes. She parted her lips and waited.

His lips touched hers. Hers trembled with all the feeling she had and dared not show. He kissed her and she did not press back, but she drew inside her all his heat, and melted in submission.

Her melting was what he needed. It set him loose to move his lips to her throat and to cup her breast. She barely arched into his hand. Her nipple rose to him of its own accord. He crushed his mouth to hers. He slipped his fingers below the deep neckline of her dress. Her nipple cried at his caress, and screamed when he squeezed. She had to tear her mouth away to breathe.

He pulled away. He stripped off the rest of his clothes. She watched him move, but could not move. Naked, magnificently so, he kneeled on the bed. He grabbed her waist, pulled her to him, and flipped her over.

Wendy lay on her stomach, her spine shivering. His hand on her nape was her only contact, the only outlet for the fire. His hand moved down her back slowly, unzipping her dress as he caressed each vertebra along the way. His touch drew her up on hands and knees; she pressed against his hand like a cat. Her dress split open and fell. She stepped delicately free of it. Her bra and panties were like pink candy. Her breasts hung like lush fruit.

Steve groaned aloud. His penis twitched. He unhooked her bra and let it fall. He pulled down her panties.

He dove for her. He fell on the bed and she fell on top of him. Wendy lay astride his thigh and wondered that her cunt did not burn a hole through his skin. On her thigh, she felt his lust like a brand.

"Are you protected?" Steve gritted out.

Wendy couldn't speak.

"Are you on the pill?"

She shook her head no.

"It's all right, I have something. Just a minute."

He rolled them over to their sides. He kissed her briefly, then pulled away.

Wendy lay on the bed. Inside she raged, but she could not move, least of all to cover her prickling skin. She needed him to cover her.

He returned, and lay on his side facing her again. He guided her hand. "It's a little cold at first." She closed her hand around the sheath. His rod in a sheath. Because he wanted to protect her. She stroked his length. She palmed his tip.

He rose and pushed her onto her back. She gasped at the burn of his eyes. But he lowered his head to take her nipple in his mouth, his teeth biting a little so that she cried out. Then came the wild softness of his tongue. She was like a volcano, his suck drawing the lava from her womb to rise and spray from her breast.

Her paralysis became unendurable. She clutched at his head, his back. She moaned. She spread her legs. He moved into position between them. The tip of his sex touched the gate of hers. The cool latex grew warm fast. She tilted her pelvis, encouraging him, near begging him, to plunder.

He entered her slowly, inch by blinding inch. Until he thrust deep at last, so keen that she shuddered. She felt herself falling into a well, and wrapped arms and legs around him to hold on.

She felt his organ enveloped in hers. In all of her. His penis pulsed, and she felt the wave in her eyelashes.

He kissed her. He kissed her hard, with a commanding tongue. Her bones softened like butter. She held onto him through will alone. But he was stronger than the grip of her thighs, and he reared back and plunged.

"Oh God!" she screamed. Again and again he plunged in her. She tossed in pounding surf until the world exploded behind her eyes.

She had to remember to breathe. She cradled Steve's spent body in hers. "I love you," she whispered into his shoulder. He lay still and did not respond. She wondered if he'd heard.

Then he lifted himself to look at her. And smiled the smile that made her shake.

"Then I am the luckiest man in the world."

He withdrew, and wiped off. When he lay back again, he gathered her into his arms. "This is where you belong," he said.

Wendy listened to his strong steady heart, and felt her own break with joy.

Don't Let Me Be Misunderstood

Claire went to Promises the next Monday night. She didn't ask Lisa to join her. All she wanted was a quiet drink after a long day at work. Good work, though. The big bosses were pleased. They'd talked to her today about a lateral move into Reservations, so she could learn that department as well. She congratulated herself; she'd be running her own hotel by the time she was thirty.

Yes, a quiet drink after work to celebrate. Which, of course, did not mean showing up at the bar in her business suit. She'd changed into tight dark jeans, platform sandals, her favorite silk blouse, and plenty of gold jewelry.

A quiet drink on a quiet night. That meant she was the only single woman here besides the old lady who talked to herself.

She bought a glass of wine before she turned and looked toward the backgammon tables. As she expected, Jackson and Eddie were there. Eddie waved her over.

"Claire!" he boomed. "How's it going, beautiful?"

"Great," Claire said. "Why aren't you guys playing?"

"We're tired of taking each other's money, aren't we, pal?" Eddie slapped Jackson on the shoulder. Jackson shrugged and half smiled. "We rounded up some new guys, oil guys from Houston who think they're hot stuff. We'll take their money for a change!"

Eddie stopped when he noticed neither Claire nor Jackson paying him much attention. "Hey, Mike! Where's

41

that cute new girl tonight?" He walked off and left the two staring at each other.

Claire spoke first. "Eddie's quite a character."

"He's all right," said Jackson. "He's happy, anyway."

"You're not?"

Jackson half smiled again. "You want to give me a reason to be?"

"Gloomy, and a smart-ass to boot. I can hear the Sisters at Sacred Heart clucking their tongues at you now." Jackson's eyebrows went up. "Toni told me you went there too," she explained.

"The Sisters!" Jackson scowled. "They were forever exhorting me to 'love God,' but turned a blind eye to the torture the popular kids inflicted on everybody else. If I dared look happy for one minute, some dumb jock was sure to come along and kick it out of me."

"The girls picked on me too."

"You?! You look like you'd fit right in." Jackson's glare was a hungry one.

So is that why you're interested in me? Claire wondered. But aloud she said, "I didn't back then. My mother worked in the office, so her kids could get free tuition and a decent education."

"Your mother worked there?"

"Yes. And mothers in our circle weren't supposed to work, except for charity of course. But then fathers weren't supposed to die suddenly and leave their families with nothing." Claire shut her mouth. She hadn't meant to say that. She didn't tell people that. Why had she told him?

Jackson briefly touched her hand. "I'm sorry. How old were you when it happened?"

"Thirteen." She pulled her hand away. "Ages ago."

She saw the old lady standing and dancing now, turning in slow, stately circles.

He continued looking at her with soft and curious eyes.

"But thank you," she said after a minute. She lit a cigarette. He already had one going, but he didn't offer her a light. "So, how about you? Is this all you do for a living? Gamble?"

He shrugged. "Most other people are stupid. And stupid people should have their money taken away from them."

"Sometimes those people take your money," Claire said.

"Sometimes. But stupid people believe in luck, and I don't. So I can't lose in the long run. It's all a matter of probabilities."

"You don't believe in Lady Luck? I thought all gamblers did."

"I'm not your typical gambler." He looked away from Claire's scrutiny to scan the other people in the bar.

"I can see that." Claire studied Jackson's face. His mouth appeared self-possessed, almost smug. But she would bet his eyes still looked starved.

"Luck, Fate, God — it's all superstition."

"There might be comfort in that," Claire mused. "That this is all there is, that this is all we are." Her mother, when not working, had spent the years since her father's death praying on her knees. She said she'd found comfort there, but Claire had never seen it help any.

Jackson turned back, his eyes deep into hers again.

"Jackson!" Eddie shouted. "Our good buddies from Texas are here!"

"Be right there!" Jackson called back. He turned to Claire. "I have to go. Will you watch the game?"

"Why? You don't need a good luck charm."

"Yes, but you look good. You'd distract the other players."

"If I can't distract you, what's the point?" Claire play-pouted her lips.

Jackson laughed. It was a harsh sound. "Maybe you could."

"And you could play for hours. I'm not waiting around that long to find out."

"But I will see you again. Soon." Jackson pulled a lock of Claire's hair through his fingers.

Claire closed her eyes briefly. She breathed. "You know you're not exactly my type."

"What is your type?"

"Rich, pretty boys I can wrap around my finger," she said.

"Don't they bore you?"

"Maybe." It was Claire's turn to shrug. "How about you, what's your type?"

"Cheap and easy!" He sobered and said, "No, not really. But no one like you. No one ever like you." They looked at each other, his hand still poised near her hair.

"Jackson!" Eddie shouted.

"I have to go," Jackson told Claire.

"Yes." She walked away before he could, and smiled to herself as she felt his eyes follow.

Be My Lover

Jess got smart fast. No more fancy dresses, no matter how good they made her feel, or she'd waste all her extra cash on clothes. Instead she created her own "uniform," a black skirt with high side slits, with a few slinky tops. Tonight she wore a blue satin halter she'd made by tying together a couple of dime store scarves.

The guys who hung out at the end of the bar stared at the knots that kept the scarves on her breasts.

"Come here, darlin'," said Tommy. He did what the guys wished they could, and gave one knot a playful tug. Jess slapped his hand away, laughing. The slap was for show; she didn't mind Tommy's touch, and the knots were doubled. They weren't coming loose that easily.

The guys, Tommy's friends and fans, were there most nights, drinking beer and only occasionally talking to a girl other than her. A couple of them, Richard and Zeke, were real cute, but none of them had much confidence.

"When are you guys going to get a date?" she teased. "You're too much man for me!"

"All the pretty girls want to dance," Richard said, while the other guys blushed and grinned. "And I don't know how."

"Well, come here, and I'll give you some pointers." Jess set down her tray and pulled Richard from the barstool. The others watched avidly. "Look in her eyes. Then she'll see your face and not your feet. Small movements are better. Don't try anything fancy! A simple sway is fine." She put her hands on Richard's hips. "Good! Now swing

45

your arms, not too much. In time to the music! Listen to the music. There you go. You're getting it!"

He wasn't, but it was time to make another round. Jess picked up her tray. "Just pay attention to her; how she moves will tell you what she wants."

She wove her way into the thirsting crowd, her tray held high above her head. She'd learned not to carry it at arm level, after a sudden fling of one dancer's hand had knocked her full tray into a slush of glass and ice on the floor.

She saw Lisa wasn't dancing, but sat at the front tables with her friend Claire, playing backgammon. Jess wished she could say hello, and thank Lisa again for turning her on to this job. What a way to make a living! Flirting and partying were two of her favorite things. She couldn't believe her luck in getting paid for it. Jess had been so busy lately, though, working the two jobs until they'd replaced her at the diner, that she hadn't seen Lisa for days. But if she went up to the table, Toni would see it as moving in on her turf. Jess only served those tables on the less busy weeknights, when just one waitress covered the entire floor.

At another ebb in the flow of the night, Jess stood at her station at the end of the bar, sipping a rum and coke. She'd asked Tommy for a plain coke. The waitresses weren't supposed to drink on duty. Was he trying to get her drunk? Was that his way of making a move? She'd been ready for a move from him since her first night!

A guy she hadn't seen before approached her.

"How much does it cost to go out with you?" he said.

Jess stared at him. "I'm not for sale," she said coldly.

"Oh, come on. How much? Fifty? A hundred?"

Jess made that much on a good night. While she enjoyed herself. She couldn't imagine any amount of money that would make her want to spend time with this jerk. Jesus, Mary and Joseph! She turned away and hoped he'd get the hint and leave.

He didn't. He put his hand on her shoulder. "Hey, I know what you girls are, so don't play the prima donna with me just to up the ante. One fifty and that's it!"

"You're barking up the wrong tree, bud," Tommy interjected. "Try the other one."

"I like this one." The guy reached to hold Jess with his other hand as well.

Tommy stopped smiling. He reached over the bar and grabbed the guy's neck and squeezed. "Can it, or get out. Got it?"

"All right, all right. Jeez!" The guy walked off, rubbing his throat.

"Sorry about that," said Tommy.

"Oh, don't you apologize! Thank you for looking out for me. Again," Jess said.

"Some guys just don't know any better. They don't know a good girl when they see one. Maybe they think there aren't any."

Jess smiled. "You know, some girls say the same thing about guys, that none of them are any good." Jess saw Tommy's face pull in. Someone must have said it to him. She continued. "It's sad, you know, when people feel that way about each other." She leaned across the bar and kissed Tommy on the cheek. "You've been real good to me."

Tommy's buddies hadn't heard the conversation, but they saw the shove-off and then the kiss. They whooped and called out the usual. Tommy and Jess smiled, softly at each other, brashly at the guys, and they went back to work.

It had to be the longest night on record, past four o'clock before Jess punched out. A fresh drink was waiting for her at the bar when she came back to pick up her purse.

"Stick around?" Tommy asked. "It won't be long until I close. Maybe we could go someplace after."

"I'd like that." She sat on one of the freshly emptied bar stools, slipped off her shoes and sighed. "Ah! It feels so good to get off my feet!" Tommy smiled. She thought she saw a line about "getting her off her feet" on his lips. But he didn't say it and she was glad. It was like him not calling her darlin'. Sometimes what he didn't say meant more to her than what he did.

The doors to Promises were shut and locked. Jess and Tommy walked to his car. "So where are we going?" Jess asked.

"Have you been out to Lake Pontchartrain?"

"Once, when I was a kid. We went to the fair on the lake shore. I still remember all the colored lights reflecting in the water. It was beautiful."

"I like to go down to the marina and look at the boats. I'm going to have me a yacht someday," said Tommy.

"Well, when you do, take me out on it, okay? I've only ever been in a pirogue. And it's not much fun when you're swatting mosquitoes and watching for gators!"

Tommy laughed. "You are something else, darlin'." He kissed Jess on the cheek. Then he started the car, and cranked up rock music on his stereo. He sped away from the curb. "I get so tired of that disco crap, don't you?"

Jess shrugged. "I don't mind. I like all kinds."

Tommy drummed the beat on the steering wheel. Jess leaned back and watched the city rush by her window.

The sailboats were beautiful, naked masts swaying in stately rows, their fiberglass glowing white in the blue pre-dawn. Tommy had brought beer. They drank, listened to Foreigner, and Tommy told her of his dream, a forty-two footer big enough to take into the Gulf and around the world. Jess listened, and waved away another beer.

"I'll fall asleep," she said. "As a matter of fact, does this seat recline?" Her head was heavy; it needed lowering.

She closed her eyes. She heard Tommy's seat go back too. She smelled his fresh beer and faded aftershave. She felt his breath on her face. And then his lips on hers. Tentatively at first, then bearing down when she didn't startle or push him away.

She didn't just accept his kiss; she welcomed it. She opened her mouth. She let him in. She teased his tongue with hers. She held his head and pressed back. She wanted a man. She wanted him. What with moving and then working so hard, her fires had been banked for too damn long.

They ate each other's mouths. They swallowed each other's moans. They kissed and kissed, not stopping to say a word.

His hand slid up and slid down. Up the slit of her skirt to her thigh. Down the swelling side of her breast. Her tightly tied top prevented his fingers from slipping beneath. He tugged again at the knot that would not give.

Their lips pulled apart as Jess giggled and Tommy cursed. She picked at and loosened the knot. But he could not wait. Over the fabric, his mouth came down on her nipple. He sucked and bit and tongued. The blue satin slicked tight against her skin. He came up gasping and staring. Her erect nipple was perfectly outlined; it was a mouthful.

"God, you're beautiful." Tommy groaned.

Jess untied the scarves. She cupped and held her breasts with her hands. "Do the other one," she whispered.

He grinned. "You're fucking incredible," he said. Then he obeyed.

Jess swam in a happy haze. Tommy's tongue felt so good. He was making up for lost time.

He stopped, and she gasped at the sudden cool on her taut nipples. He stopped to climb over the gearshift and lie on top of her. Jess opened her legs. The haze thickened to thunderclouds. She arched into him. He ground into him. Mouth to mouth again, and crotch to crotch, they ate each other up. She could barely breath and she didn't care.

She heard a car door slam. She moved to cover herself, and tumbled Tommy onto his side. "What's that?" she asked.

"Nobody," he said. "Some early riser going to his boat. Out on the lake is a great place to catch the sunrise."

"What if he sees us?"

"So what if he does?" Tommy nibbled her ear. He put his hand between her legs and fluttered his fingers. He drummed her, hard, harder, then lightly again. Her soft screams followed the beat. Lust sizzled in her like lightning. Storm on the water. So what, so what, if someone saw. Sex was a good thing. A really good thing. Jess yanked down her panties. So Tommy could touch her, could drum her, from the inside.

His other hand brought hers to his cock. She wrapped her fingers around it and squeezed. She loved how it squeezed back.

Suddenly Tommy was back on top of her. She spread wide, seized his buttocks and pulled him all the way in, in one deep and jolting thrust that broke all bounds. She writhed and cried out to God. She gripped him and clenched him. He bucked and thrust. He pounded her into her seat, and she pounded back with all that she had. Then, with more than she knew she possessed.

After a while they sat up, and saw the sunrise and a couple more sailors preparing to cast off. Her cheeks flushed deeper and Tommy grinned at her, triumphant.

Later at home in her bed, she wondered if she should feel ashamed if someone saw her. It wasn't like she'd never done it in a car before, but always parked someplace more private. Did this make her a bad girl?

But she didn't feel bad. She didn't feel bad at all.

Summer

Hot Child in the City

Claire has no more time for me, Lisa thought. *Doesn't even matter that she's not dating anyone right now. It's the job.* Her career, Lisa corrected herself. She started to heave a sigh but stopped. She knew she missed Claire more than she should. They weren't little girls anymore. It still hurt Lisa to think of her old friend Cathy from sixth grade, who dumped her after a boy found a poem Lisa had written for her. The teasing had been too cruel. It was Lisa's fault; she should have known better than to bring those feelings to school.

Lisa felt strange, dressing to go out with Jess tonight instead, though it wasn't like Claire would mind. Jess had invited her to dinner to thank her for telling her about the job at Promises. Lisa put on her Gunne Sax lace blouse and a long full skirt. Her makeup was soft, not shiny, as befitted the delicate maiden. Her cheeks had only the slightest blush. In old stories, that mild color would fade to ash before the maiden's tragic end. Claire could see herself at thirty, at forty, as a successful busi-nesswoman. Lisa could not see her life go on as far.

But tonight, anyway, she would have a nice dinner. Jess was at the door. She looked so stunning in a black cock-tail dress and room-illuminating smile that Lisa had to smile back.

She felt a hundred eyes watching as they entered Com-mander's Palace. The sweet and the spicy, two young women together in a room full of older couples and busi-nessmen. Even the formal maitre d' quirked his stiff upper lip. Jess was like a rose; she soaked up the atten-tion and bloomed all the brighter. Claire would have been regal, accepting regard as her due. Lisa pretended she could not be touched by it, by so many eyes like insects on her skin. But at least it must mean she was pretty, to be stared at so.

The women were seated. Jess ordered champagne and crab cake appetizers to start.

"Jess, it's too much! All your hard-earned money..."

"A celebration should be worthy of the name. I'll eat red beans and rice for a month if I have to. Tonight we'll have anything we want."

The waiter poured the champagne. Jess and Lisa lifted their glasses. "To good times," Jess said.

She downed the wine like a shot, so Lisa followed suit. "No fireplace nearby to toss our glasses into," said Jess. "So we'll just have to refill them."

The bottle was half gone and they were giggling like schoolgirls before the food arrived. Jess told stories from a childhood Lisa could not imagine. Sleeping two or three to a bed and making toys from tin cans. Lisa thought of her bedroom back home, and its shelves full of glassy eyed dolls not made for play.

She shook herself. That was the past and she'd left it behind. The present was this sparkling wine, this delicious food, and her beautiful, laughing friend.

The waiter approached their table with a second bottle of champagne. "Compliments of the gentlemen," he said, indicating two nearby suits with a nod.

Lisa looked and quickly glanced away. Her face flamed. Those men were old enough to be her father! How dare they ply young girls with alcohol! "Jess, we can't accept that!" she cried. "Next thing you know, they'll be coming over and sitting beside us and putting their lecherous old hands on our knees."

"Oh honey, you worry way too much." Jess patted Lisa's hand. She said to the waiter, "Tell them thank you, it's kind of them to offer, but we are doing just fine on our own." She smiled at the men, and turned back to her friend. "Now don't mind them. How about some dessert?"

Lisa ordered chocolate mousse but her skin still burned. She knew the men were watching them yet. Jess chattered on undisturbed. And she wasn't acting. She was so open, how did she keep from being eaten alive? Claire had glamour to protect her, and Lisa pretended the same. But maybe Jess was right. Maybe she just worried too much.

After dinner they stopped by Promises. It was eight-thirty, still early, and Wendy was behind the bar. She detached herself from her circle of admirers and came to greet them. "Hey, Jess! Hi, Lisa. What have you two been up to? No good, I hope."

"Hey, Wendy," replied Jess. "We just had the most wonderful dinner. How about a couple of Brandy Alexanders to finish it off?"

"Coming right up!"

Lisa and Jess sat at the bar, in the seats between Wendy's regulars and an elderly woman who sipped her drink with eyes closed, and swayed to some music that was not playing on the disco's sound system.

"That's Lola," Jess whispered. "At least that's what Wendy and I call her. From that song, you know. Can't you just imagine?"

Lisa could imagine. *That's who I'll be when I grow up*, she thought. *A pitiful old crone who can't find a decent dance partner to save her life.*

"Here you go!" said Wendy. She waved Jess's money away.

"I've never had a Brandy Alexander before," said Lisa. "Are they good?"

"Delicious. Like a chocolate milk shake with a kick."

"Too sweet for me," Wendy said. She leaned forward, her next words for their ears only. "Guess what? Steve and I are moving in together!" She grinned from ear to ear.

"Wow, Wendy! I'm so happy for you!" Jess said.

"Congratulations, Wendy."

"You must be so excited!"

"Have you found a place yet?"

Wendy laughed. "Thank you, I am! And we haven't. He was out looking today. So I'll hear something tonight."

Her voice grew soft. "I've wanted my own home for a long time. I didn't realize how much. But a real home…"

Lisa's heart squeezed. "You must love him a lot," she said.

Wendy's smile was radiant. "I do. I've never met anyone who is so strong and yet so tender. He just wants to take care of me and make me happy." She glanced up as a few new people came in the door. "Oh, got to go. But don't forget! I'm going to have the biggest housewarming party you ever saw, and you're invited!"

Lisa watched the glow remain as Wendy went back to work. Wendy's happiness, her being in love, protected her.

"Have you ever been in love, Jess?"

"Lots of times!" She laughed.

"I mean like Wendy and Steve."

"I don't know. I've never wanted to move in with anyone. I'm too glad to have my own space for once."

Lisa watched Wendy work. "She seems so happy."

"She does. So I'm happy for her. I just hope it lasts."

"You think it won't? That their love isn't real?"

"Oh I didn't mean that! It's real enough. Just look at her!" Jess paused. "I don't know. It's just that Steve can be such a stick sometimes…"

Jess suddenly squealed. Tommy had come up behind and wrapped his arms around her. His lips nibbled down her neck from nape to shoulder.

Lisa gasped. Tommy was so close she could hear him breathing. She watched his hands slide across Jess's skin. She saw Jess arch her back in response. She saw her nipples harden beneath the slinky black fabric.

Tommy raised his head. "How are you doing tonight, gorgeous?" he said.

"Fantastic!" said Jess.

"Hi, Lisa."

"Hi, Tommy."

"Well, there he is. Not even five minutes late! It's a miracle!" Wendy's voice was teasing.

"Yep, here I am. Just one more kiss, and I'll be ready to go." Tommy leaned Jess backwards and gave her a loud, theatrical smack. "Okay, now I'm ready! You girls going to stick around?"

Jess sat up laughing, her face flushed. "Maybe. If you're lucky."

Lisa smiled but her heart was pounding. The inside of her ached. She wanted what Jess had. What Wendy had. Someone's hands on her skin. Someone's lips on her neck. Someone who thought she was the most beautiful girl in the world.

She stood up shakily. "Actually, I think I've had more than enough for tonight. I'd better be getting home." She put her arms around Jess's shoulders and pressed her cheek to her friend's. "Thank you so much for dinner, for everything. It was great." She let her go. "I'll see you soon, okay?"

"Okay. Bye, honey. It was great, wasn't it? What a wonderful night!"

Lisa lay in her bed, unable to sleep. She kept seeing Jess's body, Tommy's hands. Jess loved sex. Claire loved sex. They loved what their bodies could do. Lisa hugged her pillow to her breast. *Claire would tell me I need to get laid,* she thought, by a lover who knew how.

But she wanted more than that. She wanted the full fantasy. A lover who was her Beloved.

She'd imagined him a thousand times. His dark, deep-set eyes, eyes that knew her soul at a glance. His dark hair, softly curling like a child's. His chest, wide enough to pillow her head. She rubbed her head against her pillow, imagining it was he. And tilted her head back for a kiss, from lips that were full and tender. She pressed her lips to the cotton fabric. She opened her mouth. His kiss would deepen until she felt it in thrumming in her entire body.

That was as far as she ever went. But tonight she needed more. She crossed her arms to hug herself, and drew her hands down her sides. Pretending they were his hands, caressing her gently, now sliding over her breasts. Her nipples tingled. She frowned, feeling the reaction in her palms as well. She was only supposed to feel one side of this. Otherwise her lover wasn't real.

He wasn't real. Of course he wasn't. Her hands fell to the bed. She'd be crazy as Lola before she was twenty-five at this rate. She already didn't know how to be normal. She punched her pillow and wanted to cry. And her stupid body still ached.

She knew some girls touched themselves there, and there wasn't anything wrong with that, but it wasn't something she could do. She put her pillow between her legs and rubbed up and down. And her lover came back, a glow in his dark eyes just for her. They were riding a horse together across a windswept moor, she in front, he behind. His warmth so close behind her, his arms around her, the horse rising and falling between their legs. Rising and falling. The horse running faster and faster and faster. Her lover holding her so tight! Oh! Oh! If only her lover would take her now!

But he wouldn't. He couldn't. She stopped. She was alone and sweaty and not going anywhere. Lisa turned her face into her mattress, clamped her teeth in the sheets, and sobbed.

Could It Be Magic

Claire opened her enameled case, drew out a cigarette and raised it to her lips. A flame appeared in front of her. She leaned into it, inhaled the warm soothing smoke, then exhaled and smiled.

"Thank you, Tommy. You are ever the gentleman."

Tommy grinned. "Have to take care of the ladies!"

"And you do it so well, too," said Jess. Tommy laughed and left to serve another customer. Jess turned to Claire. "It looks like Lisa may have a new beau. That's the third time she's danced with that guy tonight."

The two women gazed at their mutual friend.

"She's a good dancer," Jess said. "You can see how she loves it."

Claire nodded. "She's beautiful," she said softly.

Jess hefted her tray. "Well, it's time to make another round. Catch you later."

Claire swiveled in her seat, away from the dance floor and looking towards the backgammon tables. She was far enough away that Jackson would not see her watching him.

The sight of his face brooding over the board and his graceful, deliberate fingers had become familiar to her, but the fascination they exerted, she could not explain. Playing the game he was intense, alive. When he was not, it was as if he cared about nothing. She needed, suddenly, to change that.

He lost the game. His first loss all night. Another player took his place, and Jackson headed for the bar. Claire shifted, and watched Lisa dance. She felt him slide between the bar stools to stand beside her. She straightened, lifting her chin and her breasts, but did not turn.

"Your friend is like a flower," he said. "Soft and delicate."

"Yes."

He waited, as if expecting her to say more, to ask what about her. But she would not fish for compliments from him. She would turn to him, her legs brushing against his.

He smiled. "You are not soft."

"No." Claire laughed. She passed the test, if test it was.

"You are more like a jewel, precious, brilliant and hard." He leaned to whisper in her ear. "But a jewel with flame at its heart." He drew back. She could still feel where his breath had been, and the chill of it skipped down her spine. She looked then, fully into his eyes.

"You are more than merely pretty," he said. He leaned into her again.

"She walks in beauty, like the night, of cloudless climes and starry skies; and all that's best of dark and bright, meet in her aspect and her eyes."

"Byron," Claire said. "My favorite." She didn't know she had a favorite poet until now. Thank God something of her English class had stuck in her head. The chills were deepening, echoing in her now. And the thought that he had memorized those lines to get to her did nothing to stop them.

"Mine too. It was a better time to be alive then."

Claire frowned. What time could be better than now? This moment?

He did not see her face, and Claire forgot her pique. For he was looking at her hand, and his. He ran his forefinger along her skin, from her wrist to fingertip, as slow and deliberate as his backgammon moves. Then tip to tip he held it, a single point of contact for the forces raging between them. In all her experience, Claire had never felt so erotic, so focused, a touch.

"I want to take you to my favorite place. Will you come with me?"

"Yes," said Claire. She followed him from the bar without another word.

He drove to Riverview, an open lawn at the far end of Audubon Park. Still silent, they left the car and walked up the long, grass-clad hill of the levee. The summer night was muggy and warm, and Claire didn't appreciate making an exertion without any air conditioning to cool her sweat. "Ladies perspire, dear," she heard her mother's voice in her head, "and then they stop what they're doing and fetch a fan and lemonade." But she said nothing to Jackson. He had gone remote again, and the few feet between them felt like a chasm.

Atop the levee, he stared down at the water. The Mississippi rushed endlessly by, just a few feet below. The city on the other side was three times as far away. Claire shivered in the heat.

"One break in this and the town would wash away," she said.

"One step and you and I would be swept away. It'd be easy to drown here." There was a raw look on his face she didn't like.

"Oh maybe not. We could just get tossed up against the next pier."

He turned to her and nodded briefly. "You've got a point. I suppose we'd have to make sure that didn't happen."

This has got to stop, Claire thought. Jackson might be strange, but he was still a man. She stepped close to him. "We don't have to go into the water. We can be swept away right here."

His expression changed, but it held more smirk than smile. She couldn't be too direct, too ordinary. "Let me see your hand," she said. "I love watching your hands." She held his hand tenderly in one of hers, the other tracing it, spreading open upon it.

She held her palm against his. "I feel you. I know you," she whispered. "Can you feel me?" She moved his hand to her chest. "Can you feel my heart beat?" She stepped even closer. She tilted her head back, moving her lips into position. She parted them, about to speak again.

But he needed it to be his turn now. With his free hand he gripped the back of her neck so she could move her head no more. Slowly, slowly, he lowered his lips to hers. At a fraction of an inch apart, he stopped. She closed her eyes, waiting for the kiss she was sure to come.

After a few moments, she opened her eyes. His eyes glittered black and stark.

Claire frowned. And then he kissed her, softly, briefly. And let her go.

If he wants to play with me, she thought, *he'd better be good. Because I'll be better.*

She kept her eyes on his as ran her fingers lightly over his lips, down his chin, neck and chest, stopping at the top of his pants. She made a fist over his belt buckle and tugged. "Come on then, tough guy." She let him go, turned and walked away. She glanced over her shoulder. "So are you coming home with me or not?"

He smiled tightly and followed.

Claire walked from her kitchen into her living room and handed Jackson a bottle. "Your favorite beer."

"Thanks."

He continued his examination of the objects in her living room, picking up each book and knickknack one by one.

She raised one eyebrow. "Just make yourself at home."

"Yeah." He looked a long time at the gilt framed pictures of her family while her nerves stretched, until she yanked her favorite photo of her and her father out of his hands.

His arms came around her and he buried his face in her neck. "Claire, precious Claire," he whispered. He kissed her long hair reverently. "You are too good."

She forced his head up. She challenged him with her eyes. "Of course I'm good." She made her smile lazy. In his eyes she saw it, and she fed it, the fire that burned away the despair.

And finally it came, the kiss on the mouth that she craved: mindless, desperate, devouring.

She led him to the bedroom. He stepped heavily after her, like a sleepwalker. She kicked off her shoes, slid off her dress, unbuttoned his shirt. She got into her bed. He pulled off his shoes, shirt and pants—and stood at the edge of the satin covered four-poster. She could see him trying to control his trembling.

"I don't want this... to end too fast. It's too important to go nowhere, and too incredible to rush. Can I... just hold you tonight? Nothing more?" His eyes pled.

Her heart hurt for him. She held out her arms. He climbed in beside her and laid his head on her chest. She stroked his back and kissed his hair.

He fell asleep the next minute. Claire did not, not for some time.

Get Down Tonight

Jess counted her tips. It was a good night. She hoped the clunker she drove would last until she'd had enough good nights. She'd seen a sale sign on a '69 Mustang that looked in decent shape. It'd be six years newer than the car she drove now, at any rate.

She punched out. Tommy had a cocktail waiting for her. She sat on a bar stool, sighing to be off her feet. She slipped off her shoes, hitched up her skirt, raised and stretched out her legs. She rolled one foot slowly in a circle, then the other. Let the leftover guys look! She needed this.

One guy was not only looking but blushing. A well dressed but plain guy she'd seen a few times, he'd come in and look at the girls but talk only to Tommy. He froze when she caught him in the headlights of her dazzling smile. So Jess looked away. Poor guy. She saw Tommy nod at him as he got up to leave.

"Poor guy," Tommy said to her.

"Friend of yours?" Jess asked. There were plenty of sad cases to be found, and Tommy didn't commiserate as a rule.

"Yeah. His name's Neil. He's a nice kid. Rich, uptown family, going to Tulane, but not a bastard like so many of them."

"He seemed nice. Real shy though."

"Yeah. That's his trouble. He's got this big thing coming up and he can't get a date. All the girls he knows are girls he's grown up with, and they think of him as a kid brother, or someone to use for rides and cash when they're between boyfriends."

Tommy, catching the tilt of an empty glass from the corner of his eye, went to make another drink. Jess looked at her foot. Toes were cute just the way they were. Why some women wanted fingernail polish on them was beyond her. Especially red. It made it look like their feet were bleeding.

"Anyway, this thing of Neil's." Tommy was back, taking up where he'd left off. Jess was used to how their conversations went. "It's his twenty first birthday and his fraternity is throwing a huge party for him."

"That's nice. At least he's got guy friends if not girl friends."

"Yeah, they all think he's a great guy, though I expect they're not above taking advantage of him too." A self-righteous tone crept into Tommy's voice, and Jess smiled.

"I guess some guys make it easy to take advantage. But it's too bad."

"Yeah." Tommy paused. "But I'd like to do something for him, if I can."

"What's that?"

"Can you imagine how embarrassing it'd be to go stag to your own party?"

"Yeah. Poor guy."

Tommy leaned over and took her hands. "Jess... would you go with him?" Jess said nothing, surprised. His voice rushed on. "Just like for an hour or two. Just to put in an appearance. Just so they can see he's no loser. Please, Jess?"

If that didn't beat all! Her boyfriend, asking her to go out with someone else. No, not her boyfriend. They didn't do the relationship thing. They were friends, who enjoyed working together... and having great sex. Still, Jess hadn't been going out with anyone else, and it felt strange.

"Please? I know it's weird, me asking you."

Jess shook her head. Not saying no, but amazed again. Sometimes she and Tommy were so alike.

"But Neil was too nervous to ask you for himself," he said.

Then again, she laughed, maybe they weren't.

"I'd count it as a huge favor. I just don't want to see the guy humiliated. What do you say?" He turned on his most winning smile. Jess had one of those too.

"Okay, fine," she said. She'd never been inside one of those fancy frat houses she'd seen near the university. Like mansions they were, with columns and beveled glass windows. She guessed she'd go have a look at one. "But then I want something special from you tonight!"

"Anything you want, baby. You know I'll do anything you want."

Neil picked her up for their date in a Cadillac.

"Wow," said Jess. "Is this your parents' car?"

"No, it's mine. I like having a big car, because I can fit more of my friends in it."

That was more words than he'd said when he'd come to her door and barely introduced himself. Maybe simple questions about anything besides what the two of them were doing would get them through this. "It's nice."

"Thank you," Neil said. He opened the door for her and put out his arm, should she want to use his support in seating herself. "You look real pretty." He blushed and went quiet again.

"Thanks." She'd bought another new dress for tonight, a sweet floral thing different from her usual barmaid attire. She figured she ought to do this right. She didn't want his friends thinking he'd hired a hooker.

Stately from the outside, from the inside the frat house was just another teen hangout. The walls were paneled in dark gleaming wood, but then covered in paper and poster paint. It was dark and noisy and smelled like beer, piss and smoke.

Boys yelled out Neil's name when they saw him. Five of them rushed around him, slapping him on the back, pressing plastic cups of foamy beer into his and her hands. They eyed her, whistled and nudged elbows. "What a fox!" "Yowza!" "Way to go!" Neil grinned like a big kid. No one bothered with introductions.

"I'll show you around!" Neil shouted into her ear. Jess nodded and slipped her hand into the crook of his offered arm.

He squired her through the main room, into the dining room, kitchen and billiard room. The noise throughout made it impossible to carry on a conversation. Neil seemed almost confident, being on his home turf and not having to talk. He gulped one beer and then another, waved and shouted, and kept her by his side. A few girls came up and wished him a happy birthday, ignoring Jess. Well, not completely ignoring, since she noticed them looking her over before coming up to Neil.

"Shall we dance?" he yelled, after they'd made the circuit.

"Yes!" she yelled back.

He was no great shakes as a dancer, but she was glad to have something to do. At first anyway. They'd separated, as it wasn't a slow dance, so she was no longer right by his side. Other guys, dancing with beer still in hand, continued to shout at her date and sock him in the arm. Soon it seemed he was dancing more with them than with her, with his gang of wild boys. The girls, who were ostensibly their partners, grouped together themselves. The space around Jess felt like a spotlight.

Not that she cared what these silly kids thought of her, but it wasn't fun anymore. She kept up a good face, she kept on dancing, but it became work. And not near as enjoyable as her real job, where at least she had friends.

She persevered through another beer and another dance. Until Neil felt bold enough to put his arm around her shoulders, and slosh the contents of his cup down the front of her dress.

"I'm sorry! I'm sorry! I'm so stupid." Neil grabbed a napkin and dabbed it at her chest while his friends hooted.

"Stop. It's okay." She grabbed his hand in hers. "Will you take me home now?"

"Sure, sure."

They took their leave through more winking and hollering. When Jess emerged onto the great portico, she breathed deep. The swampy night air had never smelled so good.

Neil was quiet on the ride back, except for apologizing at every stoplight. He parked in front of her apartment building and pulled an envelope from his pocket, pressing it into her hand.

"What's this?" she asked.

"Just a thank you," he said. "I really, really appreciate it. I know you didn't have to do this, and… it made my night. You know, two of the girls even flirted with me a little, after seeing me with you." He blushed again, though his face was so flushed already it was hard to tell. "This was the best birthday I've ever had."

"You're a sweet guy, Neil. Happy birthday." Jess gave him a quick kiss on the cheek and got out of the car.

Home, sweet home! Jess stripped off her soiled dress, put it in the sink to soak, and hopped into the shower. After combing out her hair and putting on her nightie, she picked up the envelope. It was nice of Neil to write her a thank you note, and she was glad he had such a good time, but she still wasn't going to do that again anytime soon.

There was no note in the envelope. Instead there were four fifty-dollar bills. She stared, then crumpled them in her hand and tossed them across the room. He did think he was hiring a hooker! And Tommy, damn him, was her pimp! Damn them both to hell!

She refused to cry, and screaming might disturb the neighbors. Oh hell, she was too tired for this. She crawled into her bed and closed her eyes.

Two hundred dollars. That was a lot of money. It meant she only needed six hundred more to get the car. And what had she really had to do for it, but baby-sit an overgrown boy.

Brick House

"Hi, Mom, it's Wendy." She twisted the new phone cord around her fingers, warping it out of its original tidy coil.

"Wendy! Where are you?"

"I'm still in New Orleans."

"So you're not going on to California? Are you coming home?"

Wendy took a deep breath. She shut her eyes. "I am home, Mom."

"What?"

"I am home. I'm staying."

"What do you mean?"

"You remember last time I called I told you about Steve?"

"Yes."

Wendy could almost see her mother's lips thinning. She took another breath. "We moved in together."

"You're living with him?! How could you? Are you getting married?"

"No, Mom. Not right away."

A tirade followed. The one about not buying the cow Wendy had heard too many times before to listen to now. "I've got to go now, Mom. I'll call you later."

She hung up. But she wouldn't cry. She couldn't talk to her mom, not since she was twelve and grew the breasts. After that everything became a lecture about evil boys, and the mom who'd played and sang to her was gone. Her mother, in reducing her to her body, had hurt Wendy more than anything the boys could say.

She coughed and rubbed her eyes. Tears did no good! Wendy knew how her mom was. She should just stop trying.

But if her mom only knew how Steve treated her like a treasure, and certainly not like a cow he could milk for free. If anything, Steve was overly protective.

Like last Friday, he insisted on walking her to her car after work, although it meant leaving his post at the door.

"I don't like the way that new guy looks at you," he said.

"You don't like the way any guy looks at me."

"I'm serious, Wendy. Something's not right about him."

The new guy, Jim, was just off a Gulf oil rig and hadn't been near a woman in a month. His eyes were not merely hungry; they were ravenous. He did sort of give her the creeps. And that night, he'd left right before she did. But still, what could happen in a parking lot where people came and went all the time? She'd protested, but she didn't mind really. She loved that Steve looked out for her.

If her mom could only see the easel Steve had given her as a housewarming gift. Wendy ran her fingers over the smooth polished wood. His hands did this. His strong and capable hands, that shaped boards into something beautiful. That made her life into something wonderful.

She had a home. Their home. Her paintings hung on the walls, his furniture stood on the floors. She shook her head to think that she might have left this city, and kept searching forever for what she'd found right here. This place had magic, and the voodoo queen's petitioners were right to believe. Steve would think it was silly if he knew, and maybe it was, but she had left thank you flowers at her tomb.

"You can't get that shit-eating grin off your face, can you?" Jess teased Wendy. "And danged if Steve doesn't look the same." Wendy had given the full tour, and the girls went back out into the yard where Steve was turning steaks over the coals.

"You should be proud of yourself!" Lisa said. "All I've got in my apartment is some furniture from the thrift store. I don't have even one poster on the walls." She frowned. Huh!" Lisa laughed shortly at herself.

"Well, I've got plenty of stuff to hang. I mean, if you want some of it," said Wendy.

"Your own art? Thanks, Wendy. Maybe I will." Lisa fidgeted. "Claire, you haven't said anything about their new house."

"Oh, sorry," Claire said. "It's great. But I wasn't thinking so much about the decor as about you two. You and Steve seem so great together. Like you fit together perfectly."

"Thanks. We do." Wendy blushed and smiled even wider.

"Well, I take my hat off to you. It's hard to find. Jackson wouldn't fit perfectly anywhere, I'm afraid."

"But you love him anyway," said Lisa.

Claire's mouth quirked up at one corner. "Yeah. I love him anyway."

"Hey!" Steve called out. "Aren't you girls getting hungry? Come on! There's lots of food."

"We're coming, we're coming!" Wendy laughed and ran to Steve's side. He slid his free arm around her and pulled her to him.

"There's my girl. Your friends having a good time?"

"They are, but I think all of them wish they could be me."

"Well, of course they do. You're far and away the sexiest."

"Goodness, I don't mean that! I mean, they wish they had what we have. Our love." Wendy hugged him and kissed his cheek. "We're so lucky."

"Careful of the fire there, babe." Steve hauled another steak off the grill and plopped it onto a nearby plate. "But speaking of which, how about introducing my buddy Cole to Lisa? He thinks she's a fox, and she doesn't have a boyfriend, right?"

"Sure. Why not? I want everyone to be happy. Let me go talk to her."

Lisa was serving herself potato salad. Claire, Jess and Tommy chatted nearby, bottles of beer in hand.

"Hey, Lisa."

"Hi, Wendy. The food looks yummy."

"Thanks." Wendy didn't know how to start. She looked over at Steve, who smiled and nodded. Lisa saw.

"You're so lucky. Steve's a great guy."

"I know. How about you? Anyone on the horizon?"

"No one special. You know how it is at the bar. Same old guys."

"Yeah. So how about meeting someone new? Someone more like Steve?"

"What do you mean?"

"I mean one of Steve's friends from his building job. Like that guy in the striped shirt. He's cute, don't you think?" Wendy tilted her head at Cole.

"Yeah, he's nice looking."

"His name is Cole. He thinks you're cute too." At that moment Cole looked up at them, smiled shyly and looked back at his feet. "Do you want to meet him?"

Lisa looked over at her friends. Tommy had his arms around both Jess and Claire and all three were laughing. She turned back to Wendy. "Okay," she said.

"Great! Come one, I'll introduce you."

Wendy stayed by Lisa and Cole just long enough, she thought, to get them started. She left them smiling at each other, and if the conversation wasn't sparkling between them, neither was it stumbling. She went back to Steve. The steaks were all cooked and he was kicking back with a beer.

"There," she said. "I've done my part. And now, I'm starving. You got one of those steaks for me?"

Wendy settled into her picnic with pleasure. Her lover was by her side, warming the length of her body with his. His cooking melted in her mouth. Their friends surrounded them, spilling random compliments on the food, the house, the day. She basked in a golden glow; she could almost see it, like sparkling dust in the air. Such an ordinary scene, to hold such extraordinary feeling. If she could only find a way to paint both those things at once! But how could she imagine trying, because that would mean she would have to move from this perfect place.

Cole walked up and sat at the table across from them.

"So what do you think?" Steve asked him.

"I don't think anything will come of it."

"Why not?"

"Well, I said to her that maybe we could get together sometime. And she said sure, to come by that disco, that she was there most every night." Cole hunched his shoulders. "Like she wouldn't want to meet me anywhere else. And you know I'm not setting foot in any disco. It's too bad... she didn't seem like she was just a bar girl. Oh. Uh, sorry, Wendy."

Wendy waved away his apology. She didn't see Steve's expression. She watched Lisa, who stood staring after Cole with a perplexed expression on her face. *That poor girl*, Wendy thought, *she didn't have a clue*.

Fall

I Want You to Want Me

"What did you do to him, Claire?" Lisa was amazed. Jackson had not only greeted her by name, but had bought her a drink too.

Claire smiled. It was gentle, not the triumphant one Lisa expected. "I don't think anyone just loved him before. Or let him love them back."

They watched Jackson play his game. He didn't look up.

"Earlier tonight, he came over. We were going to have dinner together. We made love instead."

Lisa's mood sank. But why should it? She'd listened to Claire talk about her sex life a hundred times before. She'd been shocked and cheered by her brazenness. But never saddened.

"You see the way he handles the pips? So... consciously. He touched every inch of my body like that, with the kind of intent other men maybe use on your breasts. He had all of me throbbing, from the skin of my eyelids to the spaces between my toes. I'd never felt anything like it! His hands are just incredible."

Lisa tried to play along. "So his hands are great. What about the rest of him?"

A frown passed across Claire's forehead. "He has trouble keeping it up. Not because of me, of course! But he smokes too damn much. I know you think I smoke a lot, but I'm three packs a week, and he's three packs a day."

"Oh, that's too bad!" Lisa commiserated, and felt better. Things weren't really changing between her and Claire.

"He said it didn't matter to him, as long as I was satisfied. And in the thoroughness of his attention, I certainly was." Claire blew out smoke and looked at the cigarette poised in her elegant hand. "Maybe we'll both cut back. You'd be happy about that, right?"

"Sure," Lisa responded. Of course she would be. She'd been bugging Claire to quit since they met.

"But that's enough about me. What about you? Has there been anyone lately?"

"No. No one special."

"Tell me everything."

Lisa complied, though she left out the late night thrashings alone in her bed with her fantasy world. She couldn't speak of that. Her actual encounters sounded paltry. Nothing rich and exciting like the stories she told herself. There were no adventures, and hardly an anecdote. But Claire listened. She did not glance up as new men arrived. *Jackson really must have satisfied her*, Lisa thought. She didn't think she'd ever had Claire's full attention before. That should have made her happy too.

"You need a regular boyfriend, that's what you need. Someone who'll be there longer than the next song."

"You're probably right."

"Of course I am."

Lisa smiled a little, for her friend's sake.

"Hello, love. Hi, Lisa." Jackson kissed Claire on the cheek. Claire's demeanor changed in a flash; it was like she'd risen on tiptoe. Oh, she looked cool as ever, but Lisa had spent months watching her and she could tell.

"Taking a break?" Claire asked.

"Yeah. Do you two need another drink?"

"I think I'll get my own," said Lisa. "And go say hi to Jess. See you guys."

Jess was making rounds, so Lisa ordered another drink from Tommy. Lola was at the bar again, her face like stone. But tears slid down her wrinkled cheeks.

Lisa stared, and her sunken heart shriveled. If Lola, who'd had years to work on her dreams, could not sustain them, then what chance had she?

Jess touched her on her shoulder and she jumped.

"Whoa, Lisa. You look like you've seen a ghost!"

"Oh. Hi, Jess." Lisa smiled weakly. "You just startled me is all."

"Okay." Jess didn't sound convinced, but let it go. "You're not dancing tonight?"

Lisa shrugged. "I guess I want more than that." Lisa's eyes scanned the dance floor. She saw couples that melted into one another, like they were making love so passionate no one else existed. And she saw couples trying to imitate them, but that jerked like some distant puppeteer controlled them, leaving them unable to move into the dance they truly desired. Lisa looked away and glanced around wildly.

"I want someone…" She stopped cold.

"Someone like him," she whispered. He was here. The man of her dreams.

Jess looked over her shoulder. "You mean Richard?"

"You know him?" His hair tumbled in soft brown curls to his shoulders; his eyes were deep shadows between a fine straight nose; his full lips parted softly as they sipped his beer.

"Sure. You want to meet him?"

Her hands shook. But she nodded.

"Come on, then."

Jess introduced her. Lisa. The name of a doll. Richard. The name of a king. She and he stared at each other and neither said a word.

"Uh… Lisa loves to dance," said Jess.

Richard looked at Lisa with eyes so dark one could drown there. "I'm not very good, but for the sake of the lady's company, I'd be happy to try."

The lady held out her hand and her champion led her to the floor.

He wasn't a good dancer, almost awkward in fact, but for once Lisa didn't care. His eyes were so earnest. His eyes did not let her go, even when his feet fumbled. This dance, it felt like it wasn't a game to him, this moving closer to one another, this wordless finding of each other.

When the song was over they sat and drank together, still not talking much. *They had no need for talk*, Lisa thought. She drank more than usual, to give herself something to do with her mouth, her hand. He tenderly held her other hand. And without dancing, they were one of the shining couples, the world beyond existing only as a whirlwind to set them apart. Lisa could barely breathe within the bubble. Another thing, she thought, she didn't really need to do.

Tommy called last call, and the bubble burst. Richard walked her to her car.

"Will you have dinner with me tomorrow night?"

"Yes," said Lisa. "I will."

"There's a great new restaurant at the end of St. Charles. The Riverbend. Can you meet me there at eight?"

"Meet you?"

Color touched his perfect cheekbones. "I'm sorry. I... don't drive. I can't pick you up, except by cab, but I expect to be down that way at a friend's earlier..." He squeezed her hand in both of his. "I'm so sorry. Do you mind terribly?" He touched her hand to his lips.

Lisa gasped. "It's okay. Lots of people don't drive." Lisa didn't know of any except her elderly grandparents, and this neighbor back home whose husband didn't allow her, but she didn't say that. Not to this man whose lips were softer than she had imagined. Rose petals should blush. "I can meet you there," she said.

His grateful smile warmed her like the sun. And she was sure her long restless nights were over.

Keep It Coming, Love

Another Friday night at Promises, and Jess and Wendy chatted at one end of the bar, waiting for Tommy, or for anyone new, to walk through the door.

"It's so slow. You think this isn't the cool place to go anymore?" asked Jess.

"Maybe. Things change fast in this business." The girls looked up as someone walked by. It was Steve, getting ready for his shift at the door. They waved and kept talking.

"I don't want to look for a different job, because I like it here. You, Tommy..." Jess lowered her voice. "Well, maybe not Mike." She and her friend smiled at each other. Then she spoke up again. "But I want to make good money."

"It's just one slow night. Besides, there are some things you can do."

"Oh, I know. Like the more you flirt, the bigger the tips," said Jess.

Wendy laughed. "Right! And the lower the neckline, the bigger the tips!"

Jess giggled, but turned suddenly serious. "Uh oh, Wendy. I think Steve heard that. And he didn't look too happy about it."

Wendy looked, but Steve was already heading back to the door. She shrugged. "Guys are going to look no matter what I do. So what's wrong with me getting some kind of advantage from it?"

"Hey, you don't have to convince me!" Jess said. "It's your own life! You've got to get what you can out of it."

A group of the sleek and shiny spilled into the bar and settled at a table. Jess picked up her tray, and smiled at her friend. "It's show time!"

Show time. Strange that she used those words. She hadn't thought of it that way before. It wasn't like she wasn't being herself. She'd always been flirty; even as a baby, her mama said. But now she deliberately leaned closer and touched longer and spoke huskier. There was nothing wrong with that. It made the customers happy. Mike might be a pig, but he was right about one thing. People didn't come to a bar just to drink, he said; they could do that cheaper at home.

It made Jess happy too. Just a few weeks ago she'd been so proud to send money home, so the younger kids could wear new clothes the first day of school. This job might be a performance, a game, but what the money bought was real.

Tommy sauntered in for his shift. He patted Jess on her bottom and said hi to his pals. Jess answered him back with an order for drinks.

"All business, eh sweetheart?" said Tommy.

"And aren't you?" Jess snapped back. He hadn't asked her out after work for a couple weeks. Not once. When he wasn't going out with the guys, he asked other girls instead. Hanging out together at work, with the crowd around them, just wasn't the same. She missed him, dog though he was.

Tommy grinned and shrugged. The pals standing around snickered, but looked away. Like little kids embarrassed by mommy and daddy fighting. Jess sighed.

"Never mind, guys," she said. "Just because it's work doesn't mean we can't have fun. Now how about those drinks, Tom Cat?"

The guys chuckled and ribbed Tommy about the new nickname. He set the drinks on her tray. "There you go, darlin'."

Jess looked straight into his eyes. His grin crooked a little. He touched her fingers as she took the tray.

In another hour, she forgot she thought tonight might be slow. Though there weren't so many people as usual, they were drinking harder. She hardly had time to serve a second table before the first was calling for more. Maybe it was the moon, or the changing season. The long lazy summer was over; it was time to get serious about having fun.

The recklessness infected her. Tommy set out an apology cocktail for her and she downed it in one go. By the time the crowd was slurring its orders, Jess was more than a little high herself. During a longer break, she danced in place at her station and sipped another drink. The girl Tommy was flirting with, she was the same one he'd gone with last night. And the look on his face said he was headed there again. She frowned. Tommy didn't do repeats, not with anybody but her.

A guy who'd been watching her dance stood up, reminding Jess that it was still show time. She put a smile back on and did a little shimmy just for him. He came closer.

"Would you go out with me tomorrow night?" he asked. He spoke right in her ear to be heard above the noise.

"I work tomorrow night!" she shouted back.

"The next night then."

Jess sipped and shimmied. She loved this song. Keep it comin' love... Keep it comin' love... "I don't know. Would you make it worth my while?" She giggled suddenly. Did she really say that?

"Would a hundred dollars be enough?"

Was this guy serious? "Enough for what?" Jess asked curiously.

He stammered, suddenly unsure. "Oh... uh... you know, a good meal someplace, if we go out. That's all I meant."

"That's all you meant?" Through her own haze, she couldn't see the confusion she caused.

"Whatever you want! You..." the guy took a breath. "I just think you're so pretty."

"Aw. Sure, I'll go out with you." Why not? She could use a good dinner. He was cute too, in a goofy sort of way. Scott. His name was Scott. She told him her number and sent him away.

She had to get down to some serious fun. She turned so she didn't see Tommy fooling with that girl, and set about finishing her drink.

Scott did take her to a nice restaurant, an Italian family place. Jess wore one of her slinky outfits, a wrap top and slit skirt in clingy red knit. It was one she normally didn't wear outside the bar. *So what*, she'd thought when she put it on. This is how he knows me. She felt exposed in it now.

He ordered chianti. The wine touched her more than the conversation. More than he did too, sad to say.

"What do you think of the Saints' chances this year?" Jess tried again.

"Oh, the Saints! They can't get their act together. The Cowboys will take it away again." His voice held pride; he backed the champions. Jess smirked a little inside. Adopting the neighboring team, just so he could feel like a winner.

The food was good, though. Creamy fettuccine alfredo. And Scott wasn't stingy, ordering more wine and encouraging her to have dessert. As they waited for it to arrive, he finally made his move. Using the refilling of her glass as an excuse, he slid closer along the seat of the semi-circular booth. He stretched his arm casually across the back of the seat behind her. So predictable, Jess sighed. If nothing more interesting happened soon, she would fall asleep.

She leaned back and laid her head on his arm. She glanced sideways at him through her lashes. He was warm. She felt muscle beneath her cheek, breath on her forehead. Much better. This close, he felt solid and good. She cupped her hand behind his head and pulled him in for a kiss.

He caught on quickly, she had to give him that. His tongue lashed back at hers. His arm behind her wrapped around her shoulders. His other hand stroked down her side to the slit of her skirt.

"Ahem!" The waiter coughed. He'd brought the dessert. Their lips unlocked, but their hands stayed on each other.

"Thank you." Jess smiled, all innocence. The waiter nodded curtly and walked away. She giggled. She was sorry, but some people were so stuffy. Jess stabbed some cheesecake onto her fork. "Want a bite?" she asked, offering Scott both the fork and her neck. He growled and bit down on her smooth skin. Jess squealed and popped the sweet into her mouth.

The rest of dessert stayed on her plate. Her mouth returned to his, sucking his lower lip. Opening wider, sucking his tongue, she ate as much of his mouth as she could. How hungry could she be, after all the wine and food? But she was, somehow she was. Hungry for something more.

Beneath the table, hands rubbed on thighs. Soon, hands rubbed on crotches. Squeezed, grabbed, nearly ripped. Scott bit again: her neck, her lips, the lobes of her ears. Jess was just about poised to straddle the man when the waiter reappeared, coughing louder than ever.

"If there won't be anything else!" He slammed the check on the table.

Jess fell back, halted if not chastened. "Let's get out of here," she rasped.

In the car, Scott tried to keep his eyes on the road. Jess had unzipped his pants to encourage his erection to new heights. She prayed to all the saints that they wouldn't get in a wreck. But she didn't stop. It was too exciting, to see how far she would go, and how long he could take it. After less than half a mile, he pushed her away. His mouth was slack, near drooling. His forehead beaded in sweat. Jess turned and looked out at the lights passing her by.

She felt sleepy by the time they reached her apartment. She didn't ask, but he walked her in. She wanted to lie down. But she didn't refuse him when he lay down beside her. When he got on top of her. When he pushed up her skirt and pulled down her panties. Her legs drew up along his sides, her body responding without her. From the somewhere else she seemed to be, Jess thought that was funny.

His plunge into her shocked her back. And into ferocity. She matched him pump for pump, her nails gouging his back, her voice yelling at him to do it, to do it!

To do it and be done.

He finished and rolled off her, breathing hard. Jess struggled up to the bathroom to wipe herself off. "That was great, babe. You were great." Scott didn't respond. But she saw his closing eyes snap open. Good. She didn't want him falling asleep in her bed either.

When she came back from the bathroom, Scott was gone.

There was money on the nightstand, a lot of it. More than she'd make in a couple nights of running her tail off at Promises. More than she'd make all week at the diner.

Mom, Jess thought. *Mom wouldn't approve.*

Neither would Wendy. Or Lisa. But hell, they had to have had one-night stands before. Okay, maybe not Lisa. But what was the big deal?

What difference did the money make, if she was going to do it anyway?

Macho Man

Wendy thought it strange, how colors found in her garden could look artificial on her canvas. As if the paint talked back to her, and denied reality. No red was this bloody, it said; you're making me up.

She wanted to paint the garden, as a birthday present for Steve. But her bushes looked wounded. She couldn't make them right. She heard Steve's footsteps behind her and quickly covered the painting.

"I don't want you working at the bar anymore," Steve said.

"What?"

"You heard me."

"But I don't believe you! The money is good and I have mornings free to paint. Where is this coming from?"

"Oh, it's been coming for a long time. I can't stand how other guys look at you."

"So you want to keep me locked up? Because guys are going to look at me wherever I go."

Steve's jaw shifted. "You don't need to make it easy for them. You don't need to push your boobs in their faces."

Wendy crossed her arms over her chest. "You never called them that before."

"Well, I'm sorry, but…"

"You know I hate that word. Even 'tits' is better. You promised you'd never call them that."

"That's what those guys call them! That's what I'm saying."

"No. You said it." She hugged herself. She blinked hard. "You think I enjoy it."

"Don't you? You lean over the bar in your low cut tops, and laugh about 'bigger tips' with Jess. It sounds to me like you trip on it, the power you have over men."

Wendy gasped. "You either don't know me or you don't trust me."

"It'd be a lot easier to trust you if you quit that job."

She shook her head. No. This couldn't be happening.

Steve pressed on. "I don't know why you're making such a big deal about it. I didn't think you loved the place so much."

"And I didn't think your trusting me had conditions attached."

"What do you expect, Wendy? That I can keep ignoring you playing up to some sleaze bag?"

"It's just part of the job!" she shouted. "It doesn't mean anything!"

"Exactly. That's why you have to quit doing it."

"I…am…not…doing…anything…wrong." Wendy gritted her teeth with every word.

"Yes, you are. And you need to see what it's doing to us." He paused. Wendy turned her face away and did not reply. "I have to go to work. You think about this." Steve kissed the back of her head, picked up his tools, and walked out the door.

He thinks he can walk away, Wendy thought. *He thinks he's had the last word. That we're done with this. That he's right and I'm wrong. Wrong to do what I do. Wrong to look how I look. Wrong… to have the body that I have.*

She sobbed suddenly, and it ripped through her. She could not stop, and the sobbing wracked her again and again, and his words in her ears shred her to pieces. How he could speak of her like that. How he could think of her like that. How he could walk away…

She stopped when her brain went numb. She lay on the floor on her side, her stomach heaving, her nose stopped up with mucus. She staggered into the kitchen. She blew her nose on a paper towel. On the table, she saw a vase of flowers. Flowers she'd cut from the garden yesterday. She picked it up, and hurled it across the room. The smashing of it into shards was peculiarly gratifying. Even though it made her feel like crying again.

But she didn't. She picked up the phone and dialed Jess.

"Hello?" Her friend's voice sounded fuzzy.

"Jess, it's Wendy."

"Hey, Wendy."

"I'm sorry I woke you up." Her voice still choked with tears. She thought she'd shed them all.

"Never mind that. What's wrong?"

Wendy almost lost it again. She concentrated on speaking her next words in as normal a tone as possible. "Can I crash at your place?"

"Of course you can, honey. What's going on?"

"Can I tell you about it later?"

"Sure, sure, honey. You just come on over."

"Thanks, Jess."

Wendy hung up. She looked around at this little house she loved, one wall still dripping greenish water. She propelled herself into the bedroom, with what force, she didn't know. But it had to last until she was packed and out of here. If Steve thought she was so wrong, so lacking in decency or judgment... If he didn't trust her or their love... If he didn't get what it meant for her to have to live with this body... then she didn't know what she was doing here. Their beautiful life was a lie.

At work, Wendy went through the motions, and dreaded the time when Steve would show up for his shift. What would she say to him? What did he think when he got home and found her gone? She knew she was rash, leaving like she did. But he had to know he couldn't boss her around.

The evening ticked away. Lola came back. She wore a blue summer dress as usual. Her only concession to the change of seasons was a white lace shawl as wispy as her hair. She sipped her whiskey sour and whispered to herself. Wendy couldn't catch but two words of what Lola was saying. "Little things," she said. The rest was lost, and Wendy couldn't stand there eavesdropping. She left Lola and went back to her other customers. But she wondered what the old woman was saying, and if she meant for Wendy to hear those words. Little things. Little things mean a lot? Like keeping the job but maybe not wearing the tube tops? What would Steve say to that?

Mike dropped onto a barstool. Heavily, as if it was the end of the night instead of the beginning. "Gimme a drink," he ordered. He didn't have to say what kind. Wendy poured two fingers of bourbon over ice and set it in front of him.

"So where's that famous smile? What's wrong with you?"

"Nice to see you too, Mike." Wendy moved on down the bar, adding cocktail napkins to the diminished stacks. In one way Steve was right. Why should she be working for a jerk like Mike? She twisted a firm glass on top of the stack, curving it into a spiral, the better to easily flick one out to a customer; the napkins wouldn't stick together.

The bar phone rang. Mike leaned over and picked it up while Wendy was still at the other end. When she walked back, he was glowering.

"That was your boyfriend!" He jabbed his finger at her. "He just quit! You two have a fight or something?" Wendy didn't answer, but Mike didn't wait. "Damn it! I knew I shouldn't have let you two go out. Now who's going to watch the door tonight?" He downed the rest of his whiskey, and motioned for another. "You're just lucky it's harder to find a bartender than a doorman, that's all I can say."

Wendy had thought she was numb before. Now concrete encased her. Steve wasn't coming in. He wouldn't see her.

He couldn't bear to look at her. Not when she was so obviously wrong.

Mike ranted longer but Wendy heard nothing. She did the work, she got through her shift, but she heard and saw nothing. Until she stood at the door to Jess's apartment. She leaned her head on its hard surface. Then she unlocked it with her friend's extra key. She stepped into a dark and empty space. Of course it was; Jess was still at work. Wendy stood in the living room, unable to sit down. Unable to make herself at home. She stared at her canvasses stacked against the wall. So many pieces of wood and fabric. Little things, these pieces, and they meant nothing at all.

Never Knew Love Like This Before

Lisa had never walked into a fancy restaurant alone before. She imagined shrinking before a haughty maitre d', becoming a stammering little girl again. She should have cancelled the date. She was going to, in fact, until she realized she didn't have Richard's phone number. She had only a time and place written on her calendar, a scribble that did nothing to remind her of why she'd agreed to this.

She smoothed her hands down her dress. The resilient polyester could not absorb their moisture. A couple came out and the man held the door for her, so Lisa went in at last.

She never had to face the maitre d'. Richard was watching and rose to meet her. He took her hand. "I was afraid you wouldn't come. Thank you. Thank you for coming." He beamed. He tucked her hand under his arm and led her to their table.

He poured champagne from a bottle chilling in a nearby bucket. He poured for her, for himself, and his eyes never left her face. His fathomless eyes. As deep and mysterious as the music that made her move. Her heart beat hard, a sounding of drum and bass, that bottom of a song most important to the dance.

She looked away, at the hair curling softly on his neck. She wanted to touch it, to smooth it, to bury her hands and her face in it.

Richard murmured "So beautiful," and stroked her hair. The butterflies inside her burst into flame.

They ordered and neglected the crawfish etouffee. "I am filled with you," he said. "But I can never have enough."

He only looked at her. He only touched her hand, her hair. But it was enough to leave her breathless.

She opened the passenger door for him, to take him home. He did not get in, but turned, and his arms swept around her. She turned her face up to his. That was how the dance went. Would he know the next step? His hand gently cupped the back of her head. Yes, oh yes, that was right. His unwavering eyes, delving into hers as they came near. His mouth came closer, and closer still. Oh, he knew, he knew. Her eyelids fluttered as lips slid softly, slid over, above, beneath, and between.

She surrendered, her body softening and receiving. The perfect response, and how happy she was to finally give it. This sweet kiss was her dream come true. After this, dreams would never be enough.

He let her go. She drove him home, stopping at a row of elegant townhouses.

"Will you come in?" he asked.

But she'd lost the music on the silent drive. She was about to say no. Then she looked into his eyes. They were lonelier than hers.

"Please? I don't want this night to end. Please come in. I just want to hold you." He touched her cold cheek with warm, gentle fingers.

She couldn't say no.

Inside, the place was less lovely, furnished with a couch, a stereo, and a couple crates. Richard let go of her hand to turn on the radio. Lisa did not move until he returned to lead her to the couch.

Music again, one of her favorite songs. She smiled. Another love story told in rhythm and rhyme. He kissed her again, tenderly. Kissed her back into the dance.

His hand slid down her back and she arched it. His tongue probed her mouth and she sucked it. His thigh pressed and she opened. Her partner led and she followed.

He played her like music, touching her, touching her, here and here and finally— there—until she was in a dizzying spin that wouldn't end while the high note held.

Richard led her to the bedroom. The next song began. Her clothes slipped from her body without fumbling. He stripped off his without ceasing to caress her. His skin on hers was song made palpable. She was alive because he touched her. She was precious because he said so. She was body and soul in heaven.

They lay on his bed. She trembled. She didn't know this man! Oh, but she knew she wanted him, as he wanted her.

He kissed her neck, her chest, her belly. She floated, rising, while he sank lower. Until his head was between her legs.

With a discordant clash, Lisa remembered her old boyfriend trying to do this. Because it was something sexual to do. It was on the list. She'd stopped him almost immediately. The kisses he'd aimed at her mouth had been sloppy enough.

But Richard was no awkward boy. He stroked her thighs; he murmured sweet words that she felt vibrate against her. And he moved his mouth in a way that declared he knew just where he should be. His lips, his tongue, his teeth, belonged nowhere else. She had to follow.

To follow and... to feel. Her body rocked with feeling like never before. Lisa rocked and bucked and screamed with sensation. She couldn't bear it. She couldn't follow any longer. Crescendo overtook him, overtook her, building and sounding inside her until she was thunder and thunder was all there was.

She cried out. She shook and sweated. She just had her first orgasm. It shocked her to know that only now.

Richard raised his head. He raised himself to enter her. Had he put on a condom? she wondered, but she couldn't stop him, she couldn't ask, she couldn't interrupt this miraculous dance. For a moment she held her breath and prayed — may she not regret this night. But in the next moment prayer became a foolish thing. She was already in heaven.

Lowdown

"Hey, Claire," said Lisa. "Not watching the game?" She indicated Jackson's table with a tilt of her head.

Claire shook her head. Richard offered her his barstool. He shook the cubes in his glass. "Another drink, angel? Claire?"

"I'm good," Lisa said. Her drink was still half full. Claire shook her head again. Richard kissed Lisa's cheek and headed towards Tommy at the end of the bar.

"So what's up with you and Jackson?" asked Lisa.

"He doesn't want me near him when he's playing," said Claire. "He says he can't concentrate. I think he should appreciate how I'd distract the other players. You don't see women with any class hanging around them." She stared at her lacquered fingernails holding an unlit cigarette. She sighed.

"He hasn't been doing well lately. A real streak of bad luck. And since he doesn't believe in luck, it seems like he's blaming me instead."

"That's not fair!"

"Don't you know, sugar? Love, above all things, is unfair. Win or lose, we don't deserve what we get."

"And that's depressing!"

"Sorry, hon." She sighed. "He'll get over it, I'm sure. His luck is bound to change sooner or later." She lit her cigarette. "So. Tell me about Richard."

Lisa's face lit up. "He's wonderful! He's not like any guy I've been with before." Her face flamed, and she stammered. "I… I r…really like him, Claire."

"So I see! Well, I'm happy for you. If anyone deserves to be lucky in love, it's you."

Richard rejoined the women. He'd brought each of them another drink. "Just in case you wanted one," he said. "I can't have my girl going without." He twirled a lock of Lisa's hair and kissed it. Lisa looked up at him, a silly grin on her face.

Claire said, "If you two are going to be sickeningly sweet, I'm going to go talk to someone else."

Lisa didn't blink. "I think we're going to be sickeningly sweet," she said. "I don't think we can help it."

"Okay, then. Have fun." Claire picked up the full glass and got up.

Lisa turned then, and touched her arm. "I'll see you tomorrow?"

"Sure, hon, see you tomorrow."

Claire automatically turned for the backgammon tables, took a few steps and stopped. Jackson was sitting out, glowering at the current players. He'd lost again. He hadn't come to find her between games. Claire downed half her drink and set it on Toni's passing tray. She walked up to Jackson. She knew he knew she was there. But he didn't move. "I'm leaving," she said. She had better things to do than be treated like this. Like catch up on her laundry, for one. She'd had little time for anything but work this past week, with the medical convention in house.

He didn't move. She turned and left.

Jackson's eyes flickered. "Screw this," he muttered to no one. He stalked off, following Claire out the door.

Claire lay in bed next to Jackson, not touching him. He'd made it clear he didn't want that, couldn't take that. Now he slept and she ached. If only he didn't take it all so personally! He acted as if life made less sense with every loss to an unworthy opponent. She ached to stroke his hair from his forehead. She ached for him to stroke her anywhere.

In the morning she dressed for work. He struggled out of bed just as she was leaving.

"I'm sorry, my love. I know I haven't been good company." Jackson lifted and cupped her hand. He kissed her palm. "Will I see you tonight?"

"I can't." Though with Jackson in a sweet mood, Claire sure wished she could. "There's a meeting for all the managers. I'm not sure how long it will last. I'll probably have dinner at the hotel."

"Ah!" He held his hand over his heart. "'For the sword outwears its sheath; And the soul wears out the breast; And a heart must pause to breathe; And love itself have rest.' Tomorrow then. I'll bring take-out and we'll have dinner here. Just you and me."

"All right," Claire said. "Jackson, sugar, are you going to be all right?"

"With you beside me, how could I not?"

She so wanted to believe him.

Near the end of a long gloomy day, Claire's boss approached her. "The rain hasn't let up, and it's expected to get worse. The meeting's been cancelled. The GM thinks we should all head home before the roads flood out. We'll reschedule for next week."

The drive home was horrendous. Her churning tires spewed sheets of water as high as her windows. *If I can just make it home,* Claire thought, *Jackson and I can curl up against this nasty storm. He will hold me and touch me like he used to. We'll…*

Her car sputtered and died. The river of a road began to seep in under her car door. "Damn it!" She knew this road was bad for flooding, but she'd taken it anyway because it was the fastest way home.

At least she wasn't alone. She saw a group of people pushing another car towards the median. She stepped out of hers into knee-high, cold, dirty water and waved. They helped her out too. On higher ground her car still wouldn't start. She'd have to let it dry out before she tried again. But she had to dry out sooner than that. She was shivering, soaked and filthy. Her apartment was four blocks away; she'd have to wade all the way home, and be glad it wasn't any further. She wondered if Jackson might still be there when she arrived, if he hadn't gone out to gamble yet. She'd hate for him to see her bedraggled like this. Her grooming was one of the things that fascinated him. He'd watch her pluck her eyebrows, for goodness sake.

She kept to the middle of the road, the better to avoid stepping on things she couldn't see. But a rat swimming by saw her as dry land. It clawed up her skirt and scrambled over her body, its body big as a cat, the horrible little feet, the naked segmented tail. Claire screamed. She hit it with her purse. She hit it again. She ran. She fell. The rat swam on. She flailed and cried and nearly retched. It felt like hours until she reached her street, which had managed to drain off all but a few inches of the downpour.

Jackson wasn't home, thank God. Claire peeled off her wet clothes and threw them in the garbage. She ran a bath, filling it with the hottest water and fragrant bubbles. In an hour she was reassured by her reflection. She looked like always, confident and cool. She'd soon leave the memory behind too, of those hideous, scrabbling little claws.

"Stop that right now," she told herself. She dialed the number of Promises. Yes, Jackson was there, he was playing, did she want to speak with him? No, she'd come over. She dialed next for a cab.

The rain had stopped, but the cab company was still swamped, and it was another hour before she arrived at the bar.

"Eddie? Where's Jackson?"

Eddie shrugged. "He said he'd be right back."

Claire thought she'd go to the market down the street instead of waiting. Promises didn't stock her brand of cigarettes in their machine. She couldn't take any more waiting when what she needed was tender loving care. Thank God the sidewalk was clear now. She didn't want to ruin another pair of shoes.

There was Jackson's car. With him in it? What was he doing, sitting inside?

She got closer, and then saw the woman in the car with him. His hand was on her head. Her head bobbed in his lap. She ripped open the passenger door. "You! You…

you rat! How can you? How dare you!" Claire grabbed the girl by the arm and threw her out onto the sidewalk. "Get off of him, you slut! Get the hell out of here." The girl scrambled away. Jackson hurriedly zipped up his pants.

"Claire! Claire! It doesn't mean anything!"

"Like hell it doesn't." Her voice grated through her teeth.

"You know how tense I've been…"

"Stop!" Claire screamed the word. Then she said more softly, "Don't you dare, Jackson. Don't you dare say another word."

She spun on her heel and stiffly, swiftly as she could, returned the way she came.

But she felt cold water rising to slow her and suck her under. Drowning her with every step, to wash her away, finally and forever. The ears that heard a car door slam and her name called belonged to someone else entirely.

Don't Leave Me This Way

"Wendy! What are you doing here?" Lisa stood over her. Wendy sat in the hall by the door of the apartment.

Wendy looked up. Lisa was dressed up but mussed up too; she must have had another date with Richard. "Jess has a guy over. I was waiting until he left." Everyone had a man but her. And every ounce of her ached for an impossible, bull-headed one named Steve.

"Well, don't sit out here. Come in. We can make some cocoa."

"I'm okay," Wendy lied. She was too miserable for cocoa.

"Don't be silly. Come on in with me."

They made cocoa and popcorn. Wendy had to admit it made her feel better. Hearing Lisa rhapsodize about Richard did not.

"I do wish he hadn't drunk so much though," Lisa said softly. "We were cuddled together on his couch and he just passed out. I couldn't wake him. But he helped a friend move earlier, so he was real tired." She brightened. "But otherwise I wouldn't have been home so early, and you would still be out in the hall instead of drinking cocoa. So you see, everything happens for a reason."

"Does it?" Wendy poked at her marshmallows. "Then why does it hurt so much? What's the reason for that?"

"Oh… You miss Steve. Wendy, if you love him this much, you need to go to him, and talk to him. Don't give up on him."

"If he'd wanted to talk to me, he would have already. You know he quit the bar so he wouldn't have to see me anymore."

"But you're the one who left," said Lisa. "So it's up to you to make the next move."

Wendy stared. "I'm the one who left! I'm the one who left! You're right. I'm so stupid." Tears tumbled and she bowed her head.

Lisa stroked Wendy's hair. "Oh no, don't say that. You had your reasons."

"Go talk to him…" Wendy whispered. "It can't hurt any more than this, right?"

"That's the spirit... I guess. Now how about passing the popcorn?"

The next morning Wendy got up early and drove to her old house. Steve's house now. On another morning she'd appreciate the oaks' black branching lace in the crisp clear air. But her heart stopped beating when she thought, what if he moved? What if she'd truly lost him? She breathed a couple times, got out of her car, and walked unsteadily toward the house.

The door opened and Steve stepped out.

For a long moment they just stared at each other. Wendy felt her heart rip from her chest to fly across the empty space between them. She had to get it back. She started running. He started running. In another moment, and not a moment too soon, they were in each other's arms, their fronts pushed together to close the wounds.

"I'm sorry."

"I'm sorry."

With so much more to say, the words rushed to her lips, and they rushed to his, to tell all at once. Too much to tell, and their mouths fell on each other for release. They kissed each other speechless.

He led her into the house. He led her into the bedroom. He brushed back the hair from around her face. He kissed her earlobes, her eyelids. He touched her neck, her waist. He did not, could not, take his hands off her. "I need you. Please love me again, Wendy. I know I can't tell you what to do."

Wendy clung to his muscled arms. "I'll wear different clothes to work, it doesn't matter. I love you, Steve. I need you, body and soul."

They tore off their clothes. They lay together clasping, pressing naked skin to naked skin in his big bed. He was magnetic, she was electric, and she felt her glow must be visible for a hundred miles. Her every pore sung with pure gold. "This is where I belong," she sighed. Steve growled an assent.

Then he could not hold back. He reared, half-straddled and pinned her, holding her wrists by her head. Just as suddenly, she did not want him to hold back. She couldn't bear it, not to have him inside her. Not for a second longer. She'd been so empty. She opened her legs. "Make love to me. Now."

He shifted. He poked and he poked, he found her and plunged. They both cried out, and gripped each other all over, holding on as if letting go meant falling to their deaths.

He pounded in her again and again. She clenched and held each thrust as long as she could. Every thrust was ecstatic renewal, every withdrawal, anxiety. She dug her nails in his back and his buttocks. She wanted him in her, wanted every inch of him, wanted every drop of him. Wanted him as hard and deep and close as he could be.

Then he was; she was. He shuddered and lay still. She shuddered and wept.

"Wendy, Wendy, what's wrong?" he said when he could speak.

"N…n…nothing. Nothing. I just feel… so much!"

He held her and let her cry. That made her sob all the harder. "Shhh, now. Shhh. It's all right." He murmured softly until she calmed.

Yes. Yes. Everything was all right now. She was so lucky to have a man like Steve. He wasn't a drinker like

Richard, or a gambler like Jackson, or a who-knows-what like some of Jess's dates. Steve always wanted what was best for her. He had looked out for her from the beginning, starting with that frozen drink at the bar.

She wiped her eyes. She snuggled back into his arms. She thought of the first time they made love, how he'd controlled his passion until he made sure she'd be protected. How he'd gone with her to the clinic to get the pill for her after.

Oh my god! Her birth control pills. Wendy went cold. Four days ago she'd flushed them down the toilet in despair.

She started shaking. Steve held her tighter. "Shhh... Everything's all right," he said. "We're together again, that's what matters."

Yes. That's what mattered. She touched his strong, honest face with chill fingers, and closed her eyes.

Winter

You're My First, My Last, My Everything

Lisa looked at her watch. Richard should have met her here an hour ago. What could have happened to him? Worry gnawed at her, and doubt too. Better to be as cool as Claire.

Lisa looked at her friend. She didn't know how she did it. Claire shook the dice from her cup, and showed not one ruffle that Jackson played at a nearby table.

"It doesn't hurt you to see him?" Lisa asked.

"No one can hurt me unless I say so," Claire replied. "Why should I give up my favorite bar because of some jerk?"

"I thought you loved that jerk."

"Not anymore."

"Does that really work? Can you stop loving someone, just like that?"

Claire's mask showed a tiny crack. "He killed my love for him. Just like that."

Lisa peeked at Jackson. He was scowling, and obviously losing again. He vacated his seat for the next player, and stood watching, smoking, and drinking like usual. But his usual concentration failed him, and his eyes snapped back and forth, irresistibly drawn towards Claire before withdrawing angrily. Claire wouldn't flinch, and continued her game.

She's much better at this than he is, Lisa thought, both proud and sad for her friend.

Five minutes later, Jackson stalked out of the bar.

Another five minutes and Claire said, "Let's get out of here. Are you hungry?"

"Starving. But I was supposed to meet Richard."

"When?"

"Too long ago." Pain knotted in her gut. You will not throw up, she told herself. She should have eaten something. Was Richard in an accident? Had he stopped loving her?

"Well, you're not waiting around for him anymore. You don't want to end up like Lola, do you? Sitting around forever for someone who never comes? Let's go." Claire pushed back her chair.

Lisa followed, but her mind gnawed at her. What if Richard came and didn't find her? That would serve him right, wouldn't it? But what would he think?

Outside the bar, standing at Claire's passenger door, Lisa thought she heard Richard's voice. "Lisa! Lisa! Hey, where are you going?" He ran up to her, panting.

"You're late. I was just about to leave."

"No! Please!" Richard seized Lisa's hand and kissed it fiercely. "I'm sorry I'm late, but I'm here now. C'mon, angel. Let's go out, just like we planned. It's not too late. Please don't leave me."

Lisa shot an agonized glance at Claire, her face as twisted as her stomach.

Claire sighed. "It's fine. But you call me later, okay?"

Lisa watched her friend drive away. Richard came and stood behind her. He locked his arms around her. His lips were on her neck and at her ears. Rushed whispers of love and sorry poured in, melting and confusing her thoughts. She couldn't see his face as he spoke. But he felt warm and sturdy, and she leaned on that. She leaned back on his length, his chest and thighs. His nearness started the throbbing inside her; there was no escaping the rhythm. Her body wanted his.

Her stomach growled. And she remembered how long she'd waited. "Can we get something to eat now?" she asked.

"Fat Harry's for a burger?"

"Fine."

Fat Harry's was a dive for rich kids on St. Charles Avenue. But it was close, and served food late. It was dark, lively, smelly, and looked at first like standing room only. But most of the customers were shouting about the game on the TV over the bar. Lisa and Richard waited only a couple minutes before an acrylic covered table opened up. Richard ordered beer and burgers for them both. They sat close so they could be heard, though they spoke of nothing.

Lisa gazed without focus at the swilling crowd. She recognized many people, those she'd seen at Promises before, and those she hadn't, but who were more of the same. Beneath the island of their table, her right leg pressed warmly against his left. Her beloved, her Richard. The heat bound them. A singular fire. Below the table, through clothes and flesh, they were already one. Above that they flirted, pretending not to be. As if he needed to do anything more to seduce her, he gazed into her eyes, he touched her face and lips and hair and hands, and he said the words she'd waited all her life to hear.

"I love you, Lisa. You're so special, so beautiful. You're my one in a million, my own little angel…"

Lisa's heart soaked it in, its knot swelling under his shower. She was smiling like an idiot and she didn't care. She didn't care how she looked or who was looking. She saw nothing else but him. The crowd was a roar of noise beyond their magic bounds. Nothing could touch her when she was with her lover. She dared to whisper, "I think this is happiness."

His beer was gone and he was taking a long swig of hers. Not that it bothered her in itself, but Richard set her bottle down hard, as if he were suddenly very drunk. Or as if some earlier ingested intoxicant had just kicked in. Could it be the Quaaludes he mentioned when they'd talked on the phone? She'd thought her refusal meant the pills wouldn't be any part of their evening.

"I love you." Richard's face loomed into hers, she heard a clink, and she felt cold liquid pouring into her lap. His sloppy kiss grazed her chin as she jumped back, righting her now empty bottle.

"What? Oh, sorry…" He reached for napkins, knocking the bottle over again, and setting himself off-balance in his chair. He fell to the floor.

The crowd rushed in on her. People, person after person, looking, pointing, and laughing.

Her face burned. Her hands and feet were ice. Still she helped him up. And then led them quickly out the door.

She drove. She parked in front of his apartment. She waited for him to notice where he was.

"Come in with me," he pleaded. He took her hand. He kissed her fingertips with overt precision.

"No," she said. She hardly believed she said it. The word crushed her already humiliated heart. "Not like this."

"I'm sorry, I won't do it again. I know I spoiled everything, I don't deserve you, my princess, my angel…"

Another rain of his words on her ears, a flood of them, designed to sway if not sweep her away. But the cold wet in her crotch was more urgent. She felt ill and soiled.

But he would not get out of the car, until she mashed her mouth to his and swore she loved him madly and forever. Yes, madly. Yes, forever. Yes, she'd spend the rest of her life waiting in a bar for him if that's what it took… yes, yes, yes.

But no. Driving away in tears, Lisa thought, *maybe no.*

More, More, More

"Thanks for coming, Jess." Neil squeezed her hand. "I'd feel like a creep going alone, but I couldn't bring a regular girl here." Neil and Jess smiled at each other. They both knew Jess wasn't a regular girl. She was special. "And if I went with the guys… well… you know it'd be different with them. I couldn't just be myself."

Neil stopped in the middle of Bourbon Street, making the revelers directly behind him stumble and curse. "I mean it, Jess. You're the greatest. With you I can act how I want, and you stand by me."

"Thanks, sweetie. I like you too," Jess said, squeezing his arm. And she did. Neil was gentlemanly, generous, and took her to unusual places. He never so much as kissed her on the lips. "Come on," she said. "Let's go in."

Jess had never been inside a strip club either. *But why be shy about it*, she thought, *if that's what you wanted to do*. The gaudy entrances and the shouting of the hawkers weren't supposed to scare you away. She linked her arm through his and marched them in.

Once they stepped through the door, Jess realized why Neil needed her. His mouth slackened and practically drooled. He saw nothing but the next-to-naked women on stage. Jess gracefully found seats and ordered drinks for them both.

The club was like most bars, dark and smelly, with its male majority in various states of stupor. But here, except for Jess and one other, all the women were working. Though Jess guessed she could say she was working too.

She looked at the nearest grinding woman, into her heavily made-up, sagging face. Jess bet her body was on autopilot and the stripper was thinking more about her dinner than her customers. If she was thinking about anything at all. Jess shivered. She looked, but the soul in the stripper's eyes was inaccessible. Or gone. If she's hiding her insides from the audience, she's hiding them perfectly, Jess thought. Like Lola, she'd seen better days. Then again, Jess shivered again, maybe she hadn't.

Jess vowed she would never, ever, work in a place like this.

No, she had to be honest with herself. She knew what poverty was like. She might do a lot of things if she needed the money. So she changed her vow. She'd be smart enough and work hard enough and never ever need money that badly. So she would never have to sell her soul.

The music ended with a final clash, thrust and bang. The aging stripper tripped offstage. A slick announcer came on to introduce the headliner act.

Neil perked up and proudly ordered the next round of drinks himself.

Jess would not sell her soul. She might rent her body, but it was always her choice; she had more offers than she ever accepted. There had to be something special about the guy, something tempting in the offer. She didn't like to think of it as renting anyway (although she had to admit the truth of that), she liked to think of it as sharing. Sharing her body with nice lonely guys who liked to give her things.

The star strutted on stage. Oh, she was different! The crowd sat up and howled. Neil froze into stone, his eyes wide as could be.

The stripper was fresh, lithe, and gorgeous. Her character was a gangster girl. She wore a fedora, gloves, tall boots, and a tiny pin-striped skirt and jacket. She carried a toy machine gun. She held a lit cigarette between her pouting red lips.

But it was not just youth or beauty or costume that had men hollering. Unlike the other, she was there. The men could feel her eyes, her power, her will to engage and to enslave them through their lust. Her eyes weren't glazed; they glittered.

Jess put some bills he'd previously given her in Neil's hand. It wasn't time yet to offer them, but it gave him something to hang on to, to work up to.

The stripper's maneuvers made Jess's hamstrings hurt just looking. Had the older one ever been this brash? Had she ever enjoyed this flaunting, this animal sexual display? *I might enjoy it,* Jess thought, *if I could choose the audience.* She smiled. Her thoughts wandered on.

Would the young one become like the old one someday? She'd never dream of it, surely. And the old one? Had she seen her mechanization coming? Had she known as her soul was gnawed away bite by bite?

What did Jess see coming in twenty or forty years? What did she want for all those other years of her life? She didn't have a clue, beyond money in the bank to take care of her physical needs. But what did she want for her soul?

Neil rose, and wavered. Jess leaned against his side and he stood firm. The dancer did splits in front of him. His hand shook but he didn't drop the money. His bills were tens and twenties. They stood out from the rest. The stripper noticed and played a while just for him. Neil gaped and quivered and gave her all he had, bill after bill after bill. When his hands were empty, she pushed the muzzle of the gun into his chest. She mimed a shot. She mouthed, "Pow."

Neil jerked and came. He wasn't completely obvious, but Jess was still leaning against him. She felt the rush in his body. She helped him sit down. They drank the rest of their drinks quickly and left soon after.

In the car, Jess tried to gather her thoughts, but they fled past her like the strings of streetlights.

Neil dropped her off at her apartment, hugging her and pushing another envelope into her hands. Jess wished he held her longer. She almost wished he kissed her.

He drove off and she stood alone on the street. She lifted her eyes to the sky. If she were back home on the bayou, there would be stars.

Chain

"Jackson called me," Lisa said. She reached for some cheddar. Claire turned her head to look out her living room window. The friends were dining at Claire's tonight, and dinner was cheese and crackers.

"I was so surprised! You know he and I never said much to each other."

Claire didn't speak, so Lisa went on. "He said he'd been a fool, and you were the best thing he'd ever known. He asked me if I knew of anything he could do to get you back."

"What did you tell him?"

"I said I didn't know." Lisa paused. "Is there anything? Should I have told him something?"

"No." Claire shook her head. "He can't take back what he did. And I can't allow someone to betray me." Claire's heart threatened her throat. Freeze! she commanded it. Do not feel a thing. "He's been calling me too. He said he quit smoking for me; you know, since it affected his ability to perform. Can you imagine? He smoked 3 packs a day since he was fifteen, and he quit cold turkey."

"Wow. That must mean something."

Claire's eyes stung and she closed them. "What should it mean? What difference should it make?" She carefully touched a tissue to the corners of her eyes. "I know quitting like that is an accomplishment. Good for him. But that he can do amazing things is not the issue." She crumpled and tossed the tissue.

"I can't trust him. I don't even know him! How he could do such a thing... what went on inside of him, to ever think that was an okay thing to do... after how we'd opened up to each other..." Claire shook her head again. "I don't know. I don't want to know.

"I loved him. But I had to stop. There isn't anything he could do now. It's over. It was a mistake to begin with." Claire spoke so softly now that Lisa had to lean forward to hear. "I wasn't enough to save him. He's beyond my help. He always was. I didn't think so at first, so I guess he had to prove it to me."

"You don't think he's really sorry?"

"No. I know he's sorry. That's the tragedy of it." Claire twisted up a little smile.

"You don't believe he's changed?"

"Maybe he's trying to. I have no idea if he'll succeed. I just know I want no part of it. I can't. I can't trust him not to hurt me again. And I'm no martyr." She drew herself up in a show of hauteur. "I'm more the queen type, don't you think?"

Lisa smiled for her, and picked up Claire's hand and held it. They sat together in silence.

Then Claire stood up to freshen the drinks. Peppermint schnapps over crushed ice, in honor of the season.

"Lisa, are you going home for Christmas?"

"I can't afford the airfare. My mom wanted to send me a ticket, but dear old dad wouldn't let her spend the money on a renegade like me." Lisa gritted her teeth in the tiniest of grins. "So I'll mail some presents and call on Christmas, and talk to Mom anyway."

"I'm sorry." Claire handed Lisa her snowball.

"It's fine, really. Mom wants to think we're close, but we're not. We're just stuck with each other. It's a relief in a way."

"Well, you can't be alone on Christmas! Come with me to my mother's house. She always makes a big fuss and a fabulous dinner. I know you'd be welcome. She's great that way."

"I thought you didn't like your mom much," Lisa said.

"Are you kidding me? I love her!"

"You never say good things about her."

"I just never agree with her! We're always fighting. But of course I love my mother."

"I didn't know there was any 'of course' about love," Lisa mused.

Claire shrugged. "Maybe there isn't. Not with men anyway." But she knew her daddy had loved her. Still he had left her. But he wouldn't have cheated.

"Anyway… are you all done?" Claire asked. "Let's get out of here."

They swept the snacks that comprised their dinner off the coffee table, and headed to Promises.

"Hey, Jess, hey, Wendy, are you going to be in town for Christmas? Lisa is coming with me to Mother's, and y'all are welcome," Claire announced.

"Steve and I have plans," said Wendy. "We want to spend our first Christmas together in our own house. Thanks, though."

"And I'm going home for Christmas," Jess said. "I can't wait! I've missed them all so much."

"Would anyone like to come over Saturday afternoon?" asked Wendy. "I'm making cookie cutter ornaments."

"Sounds like fun."

"Hey, Wendy," said Jess. "Does little old lady Lola still come in here? I haven't seen her for a while, but I thought maybe she's been leaving earlier so I've been missing her."

"Just a sec." Wendy swiftly served up a couple gin and tonics for Toni and returned to the group. "She still comes in, but not so much as before. And she's quieter. No more dancing or talking to herself. She just stares. She looks sad."

"Aw. Too bad."

Claire had to smile. She had such sweet friends, to care about a strange old woman like that. Beautiful friends — dreamy Lisa and wild woman Jess and earth mother Wendy. They made quite a sight, the four of them together.

And she knew he was watching from across the room, a dark haired man with long white fingers. She knew he was suffering. Across the room, she felt the razor edge of his need. She felt it. She felt it like she had always felt him, as if they were one. To have had that… and to have had that corrupted…

Yes. She knew he was begging her now. But she was immune. Let him see her drink and laugh. Let the razor turn in his hand. Let him be cut by how little she cared.

Let him be cut, again and again and again. Let him bleed. Oh yes, let him bleed.

Shame

"What are you doing here?" Steve asked, and for good reason. He was home from work, and Wendy should be working, but she was sitting on their couch waiting for him.

"I called in sick today," she said.

"Are you all right?" He put down his tools and keys. He sat next to her and took her hands.

"Yes," said Wendy. "But I'm pregnant."

"Pregnant!" Steve shouted. He jumped up, dropping her hands into her lap. "How the hell did that happen?"

Wendy slumped, maybe she was not all right after all. "When we broke up I stopped taking the pill. I was so upset I threw them away. And when we got back together, that first time... Well, I wasn't thinking. I was just so happy to be with you."

"You're pregnant. Oh my god." Steve sank back to the couch and hung his head in his hands.

"I know it's really soon, and we weren't planning on marrying yet... but... it could work out, don't you think?" She touched his arm. She stroked his hair. She willed him to look up. She willed him to take her in his arms and tell her not to be scared, that everything would be all right.

"Wendy." Steve's voice choked on her name. "I don't want children. I never have."

"You don't want children? But we talked about settling down…"

"Settling down meant being with you. Having a home with you. It never meant starting a family."

Steve didn't look up. He didn't say anything else, or Wendy suddenly could not hear what else he said, what with a black river rushing in to fill the hole punched through her world. She said again, "You don't want children. Ever." Her voice was flattened. The river did it to her. All that dark cold weight.

Of course. He'd always been so careful, so concerned. When they talked about their dream, their home in the country, she'd always imagined a few kids running around. But she'd assumed, and never mentioned them, and he never even imagined them. Never. She deflated, her body caving over the emptiness inside, gutted like a fish. But she was still pregnant.

"I'm sorry, Wendy," he said. "What are you going to do?" He took her in his arms then. She let him. She could not move.

He didn't say it would be all right. In return she didn't tell him how she felt so utterly alone.

And she didn't tell him how desperate she became in the next hours and days. Steve was all kindness, giving her time and space to think, he said, while she sunk ever deeper. How could she think? She knew what he wanted, and what he never wanted. That wasn't going to change. So she didn't tell him when she left one morning and took the trolley to the Delta Women's Clinic.

She'd arranged for Jess to pick her up. She wasn't supposed to drive afterwards. The clinic had a big waiting room with all kinds of people. Young, old, richer, poorer, black, white—but all women, some already with children. All kinds of people, but no face she expected, because Wendy didn't know what to expect and she was more scared than she'd ever been in her life. Good thing she'd gone numb, or else she'd be screaming.

A woman with gentle eyes led her to a changing room. She said her name. Wendy couldn't remember it a second later. Brown Eyes said she'd be back in a few minutes and gave her a gown and a bag. "You can put your own stuff in here."

"Thank you." Wendy did as she directed.

The woman walked her over to an operating room. Nothing so slick or permanent as in a hospital, but unmistakable just the same. Wendy climbed onto the stainless steel table with stirrups.

"A nurse will come in and connect you with an I.V. and give you a sedative. Then the doctor will come in. He'll give you several shots of a local anesthetic in your uterus. The first one will sting. Then he'll do the D and C." The woman patted Wendy's arm. "I'll be back, and I'll be with you." She looked sincerely into Wendy's eyes. "You're going to be fine." Then she left.

Wendy wasn't left alone long. The masked and gowned nurse came in and performed her duties. She faded into the background. Was that the sedative taking effect so quickly? The masked and gowned doctor came in. He wheeled a device in with him, like a canister vacuum. He inserted a speculum and she gasped at the intrusion. What would happen if she started screaming now? She'd start screaming and never stop.

Fire! The first shot was burning fire, searing deeper within her than anything foreign had a right to be. She gasped, she couldn't breathe, she would die on this cold cold table…

But Brown Eyes was back. She had a mask on too, but her eyes held their same gentle strength. She gave Wendy a paper bag. She told her when and how to breathe in it. She held Wendy's other hand in hers. And minute after minute, Wendy gazed into those eyes and tried to ignore the pulling and scraping. She tried not to hear the sucking of the machine. She tried to remember to breathe. She had to. The eyes wouldn't let her pass out and run away.

The door swung open. The doctor was leaving, wheeling his machine away. There were bloody instruments on a tray. There was blood on the floor. Her blood. Her baby's blood. Oh god, oh god, not hers anymore.

Brown Eyes helped her up, got her into a wheelchair. She wheeled her to recovery. In the recovery room were rows of vinyl recliners, half filled with women. Wendy was helped into one of her own, and given a pillow and a blanket. Funny how the women looked all the same now. With paled faces and bodies dressed in sheets, they were like so many ghosts.

Heart of Glass

"So, did you get what you wanted for Christmas?" Tommy asked Lisa, setting a glass in front of her.

"No," she said. "But I never do."

"Aw!"

"Oh, it's no big deal." She waved a hand. "I am worried about Richard though. He never called and isn't answering his phone. I haven't heard from him in a couple weeks!"

"He probably went to his grandmother's in Biloxi. He does that when he needs to dry out for a while, and have someone else take care of him."

"He left town without telling me? To dry out?!" Her voice rose. "What the hell, Tommy?"

He looked away, almost squirming. She'd never seen him look so uncomfortable before. It might have been funny if she didn't feel like smashing his face. She threw some money down on the bar for the wine she never tasted, and stalked out of the bar.

Oh god, Richard. Her beautiful Richard had a drinking problem. And how stupid was she. She should have known! Tommy had known, but he'd said nothing. Tommy had known, and served him liquor with a smile.

At home, she lay on her bed like a corpse. *It's over*, she thought. How could she stay with someone who needed booze more he needed her? Who'd never mentioned this grandmother, yet went there for tea and sympathy, and not to her. How could she be with someone who could leave her alone at Christmas without a word?

She shouldn't cry. She was stupid, but Richard's problem wasn't her fault. It wasn't her fault that she wasn't enough for him. It wasn't that no one could really love her.

She shouldn't cry! But the tears leaked out. She tilted her head slowly to the side when her ears filled up. She wished she didn't have to move at all, or ever again. Like if she pretended to be dead hard enough, living wouldn't hurt so bad.

Still she wept, and lay there, and dully watched as the night become day. Then Lisa got up to dress for work.

She lived through the day. Now if she could just make it home. But a rally blocked her way. People swarmed in the street and on the sidewalk. People in white robes and white pointed hats. KKK! But this was the seventies! What in the world were they still doing here? And out in public! It was shameful, this part of the South's past, and horrifying to Lisa that it wasn't long buried. She'd had no idea.

She nosed her car through the crowd. Her heart pounded. Would they stop her and pull her out of her car and kill her? No, of course not, because she was white. But she sweated just the same. Who knew what these people were capable of? What kind of people were they?

She could see their faces, as they weren't masked. And they looked like... her friends, her neighbors, her dance partners. They looked normal, happy even, with no way to tell from the surface the hate that must live inside them. Her sweat chilled.

She remembered that New Orleans was over fifty percent black. So why was it she saw so few black faces in her daily life here? Back in her hometown the population was almost all white, so she never thought it strange to see no dark faces. It felt more than strange now.

She gripped the steering wheel hard the rest of the way home.

She didn't want to go back to Promises that night, but Claire wanted her company, and Lisa knew she was hurting more than she'd admit. Jess had the night off, and the three of them had drinks together. Tommy was his old self again, and sweeter than usual to her, but Lisa would not meet his eyes. She told her friends she and Richard were through.

"I think you've got the way of it, Jess," said Lisa. "Just going out and having fun and not falling in love."

"Oh I don't know about that," Jess said. "Sometimes it's not as much fun as it looks. I think I might like to fall in love. I've just got to pick the right guy to fall in love with."

"But love just happens," Lisa protested. "You can't choose."

Jess laughed. "Sure you can!"

"But do we choose?" mused Claire. "It seems like when you have a dream, and then some guy comes along who sort of fits that—you turn him into the One. Without really knowing who he is, or what he might be capable of."

Lisa thought her heart couldn't crumble into smaller pieces, but she was wrong. *Is that what she'd done? Was it all a lie, her feelings as well as his?*

Claire continued. "It's like anyone in the right place at the right time would do."

"No, that can't be true," said Lisa. "Besides, you can't tell me Jackson was just anyone to you, Claire. He wasn't even your type! And Richard... well, maybe he wasn't who I thought he was, but he wasn't just anyone to me." Lisa gulped. She was too close to too many tears. "I loved him!" And she'd thought she had no more tears left. Well, she was being wrong all over the place, wasn't she?

"I know." Claire spoke more softly, patting Lisa's arm. "And you're right. Jackson was different." Her voice turned tough again. "But whatever it was, it's done now. And I'm done with dark and brooding. I want someone

more fun. How about it, Jess? Could you spare one of
your guys?"

Lisa knew Claire was teasing. As if she'd go out with
anyone's seconds!

But Jess laughed. "One of them? I don't think so! Bar
guys are no good, any of them."

Tommy heard that as he passed by. "Hey!" he said.
"Not even me?"

"Especially not you, sweetheart. You're as bad as they
come." Tommy made a hurt face, but his chest puffed
with pride, and he smiled as he moved on.

Lisa said, "Steve's a good guy. I think Wendy and Steve
are the only happy couple I know. Though I haven't seen
either of them lately."

"She quit!" said Jess. "I can't believe I forgot to tell
you!"

"She quit? Why? Where is she working now?"

"You know, I'm not sure. I need to call her up and see
how she's doing." Jess's forehead creased into a frown.

Lisa opened her mouth to respond, and then forgot
what she meant to say. Richard walked into the bar.

"Hi there, beautiful!" he said. Oh, he was so handsome!
So perfectly, horribly handsome.

She stood up. "I have to go," she mumbled. She rushed
away before he got close enough to touch.

"Lisa! Where you going?" Richard ran after her. Out of
the bar and down the street. The air was bitter cold.

He kept talking, kept trying to catch her. "Oh, you must
be mad because I haven't called. I'm sorry, love. Some
family business came up. I had to go take care of it. You
know I wouldn't leave you unless I had to."

How many more feet until she got to her car? How many more words before she fell apart completely?

"Lisa, honey! Don't be mad. I'll make it up to you. Let's go out! Or better yet, stay in. We can get a bottle of your favorite champagne, and some chocolates…"

She was at her car door, but her hand shook and she couldn't get the key in the lock. He came up behind her. He put his hand on her shoulder. She whirled around, flinging it off.

"No, Richard. No! I can't see you anymore. Please let me go."

"Let you go? But I love you! We're meant to be together!"

"No. We're not." She turned and tried the key again. This time it worked. But he was standing too close; she couldn't open the door.

"Why are you making such a big deal about this? I said I was sorry. Come on, love," he wheedled. "Come on now. Aren't you glad to see me? I missed you so much. We've got to make up for lost time." He stroked her back.

"NO!" She yanked the door open, pushing him aside. "It's over!" She jumped in. He grabbed for the door, but a sudden fear made her strong and she pulled it shut. *My god*, she thought, *what might he do?* What else lay hidden behind that beautiful face? She hurriedly started the car.

"It's not over! It can't be!"

She pulled away, but she heard him shouting. In her rear view mirror, she saw him chasing after her, down the middle of the street.

"But I love you, dammit!" He shook his fist but disappeared into the distance when she gunned the engine.

She trembled so hard it was hard to see. It didn't stop when she got home. It didn't stop when she got into bed. She didn't stop shaking for hours.

Too Much, Too Little, Too Late

Wendy stared at the red glass ball in her hand. She could see her face in it, bloody and distorted. How fragile it was! How easily dropped, to shatter into a thousand tiny shards. But this one, this one would make it; she hung it carefully on the tree. The effort exhausted her. And there was an entire box of these to go.

She despised the look of them, their evil shining red. Still it was better, and more fitting, than the dough ornaments she'd molded but now would never paint. She picked up another ball and cradled it in her hand. Her useless hand — it couldn't hold a brush, or a child — but it could hold this brittle bit of emptiness.

She heard Steve's voice, hopeful in tone, but the words passed her by. What could he have to say? What words could bring her baby back, her life back? He wanted Christmas, so she was trying. She tried to remember joy. She tried to remember she loved him. She could barely do a thing for all this trying. She stood stiff and still. Steve touched her arm and she jumped.

"Wendy." He turned her to face him. He held her arms. "Wendy, I'm sorry. I should have been there for you. You should have told me you made the appointment. You shouldn't have had to go through that alone."

She stared at him. Of course she had to go through it alone. It would never have been him on that table with his legs spread for a machine. It wasn't his womb that was unwelcome. He shook her. "Wendy! Please say something. Please talk to me."

"What do you want me to say?" Her voice sounded far away.

"Something! Anything!" He let go of her to pull his hand through his hair. Something he did when he got frustrated, Wendy remembered.

His voice softened again. "Honey, we've got to get through this. We will get through this." He led her to the couch and sat her down next to him. "I know it was hard, but you did the right thing. We can move on now. We can build a good life together. I love you so much." His voice choked. "Please, honey. Say you'll try. You've got to try."

But she was trying. Couldn't he see that? It was just that her trying didn't get her anywhere. Despair held her too tight. 'Good' and 'life' just didn't go together anymore. Not for her. She shook her head. She struggled to speak. "I can't…"

"You can't move on from this? Or you won't?"

"I… can't…" She looked down and saw her reflection in her hand. She saw tears of blood in there. She watched them splash colorless on her chest.

"Damn, Wendy! I don't know what else to do!" Steve cried. He hung his head in his hands.

She said nothing. Silence fell like so many tears.

"We can't go on like this," Steve muttered at last, still holding his head, seeming to talk more to himself than to her. He continued, softer still. "I can't stand seeing you like this. And I can't stand not being able to do a damn thing about it. Maybe we should've just had the kid."

Wendy convulsed with pain. And her empty, useless hand clenched a thousand bloody shards.

"Wendy! Wendy! You home?" She heard the voice, and the pounding on the door. If she didn't move, the voice might go away. But she heard the scraping of the planter on the stoop, and the spare key turning in the lock.

"Wendy. You haven't returned my calls." It was Jess. She pulled back the curtains in the bedroom. She sat on the bed. She smoothed Wendy's hair. Wendy looked at her eyes. Such nice brown eyes Jess had.

"Jess," Wendy croaked.

"Wendy, sugar baby, what can I do?"

"It's no good, Jess. I can't stop thinking about it. And I can't seem to do anything else."

"Well, that's what I'm here for, hon. To help you do something else." Jess spoke gently. But she grabbed Wendy's shoulders with unexpected strength. "And what we're going to do is go out to lunch. Get you some fresh air." She sat Wendy up on the edge of her bed. "Now let's get you dressed. Where's that pretty pink sweater of yours?"

Wendy almost smiled at Jess's fussing, and she lifted her arms obediently. Jess, now, she would make a great mother someday. The near smile collapsed; the same crushing weight bowed her head. She couldn't go anywhere. She couldn't even stand.

But somehow Jess got her on her feet. And out the door into the car. The world flew by her window, blue and white and brown. Colors. There were colors in the air.

She breathed them in, and thought she might not pass out after all.

Jess took her to Fat Harry's. "It'll be nice and lively," Jess said. "And they know us there." Jess ordered burgers and beer for them both. "Plus two shots of tequila to start things off."

"Jess! You're going to get me drunk!"

"Well, better drunk than dead! But you know, you don't have to drink it." Jess touched her arm. "I just want to shake things up. Let you forget about it, for a little while at least."

The drinks arrived. Jess held up her shot glass. Wendy slowly raised hers. "To us!" Jess said. They tossed down the tequila.

Wendy made a face but managed not to cough. It had been a while since she'd had a drink. It hit her hard and quick. It had been a while since she'd had a real meal too. She hiccupped, then giggled at herself. "Better drunk than dead!" she agreed.

Soon Wendy felt as if she'd laughed more in the last hour than she had her entire life. Maybe that wasn't true, but if she looked back at her life, she could only see the pain. Jess was right. It was time to forget. She ordered another two shots.

"Ladies! Why don't you let me get that for you?" A burly man with a long mustache and sideburns loomed over them.

"Oh, hey, Dan," said Jess. "How's it going?" She turned to Wendy. "Dan's the owner of Dionysus, down on Magazine Street." Wendy looked up. His eyes were blacker than brown.

"And who's your foxy friend?"

"This is Wendy. She worked with me at Promises. Tending bar, not waitressing."

"You know I'm looking for a new barmaid." Dan pulled up a chair and made himself at home. "Are you interested?" He leaned closer. "I know I'm interested in you."

Wendy smiled. She didn't say anything. She hadn't been paying attention. She picked up her shot glass, saluted him, Jess, and the table, and drank it down.

Dan grinned and ordered another.

She didn't have to say anything. It was so easy, to let the old role come over her. To nod and smile when she should. But unlike the old days when she dreamed of paint and paper, she thought of nothing at all.

"Oh," said Jess, "it's getting late. We better go, Wendy. I've got to get ready for work."

"No. I don't want to go home now." If Wendy went home, she might have to think about that thing she didn't want to think about.

"But Wendy, I've got to go! I don't want to leave you here."

"I'll see she gets home," said Dan.

"Yeah, I just bet you will."

"Don't you trust me?" He grinned, not even trying to make it look innocent.

"About as far as I can throw you. Come on, Wendy."

"No. I don't want to go." Wendy looked pleadingly at Jess. "Please, Jess. I'll just stay a little while longer. Dan can give me a ride. You go on."

Jess sighed. "All right, hon. I'll talk to you soon, okay?" Turning to Dan she whispered harshly, "Now you be good and I mean it, Dan. If you take advantage of her, I'll have my guys put the word out to boycott your place, you hear me?"

"I hear you," he grumbled.

"And?"

"And I promise I'll be good. Jeez, Jess. For a hot chick you can be one tough broad." He stared sullenly at his beer.

"Good boy." Jess smiled and stroked his face back into an easy smile. "You won't regret it, I promise." She stood up and hugged Wendy goodbye. "Now you call me, at work or at home, if you need anything."

"Don't worry about me, Jess," said Wendy. "I'll be fine now. Thanks for everything."

It was true, Wendy thought. She would be fine, now she knew what to do.

Mardi Gras

Disco Inferno

"Throw me something, mister!" Jess belted out. She flashed her smile and the satin-clad misters did as she said. The crowd surged, grasping with a hundred hands. They knew, on this day of all days, that doubloons and bead necklaces could save their lives. Lisa had already had two tug-of-wars with costumed strangers and the parade had been going for just ten minutes.

Though Jess encouraged her, the yells Lisa managed sounded feeble in the rowdy crowd. One thin girlish voice lost in the great roar. Still, she shouted to them with the rest. And whether they heard her or not, they noticed her. They winked, they waved, and they tossed strings of beads by the handful.

One man blew Lisa a kiss before his float passed by. And for one impossible moment, her eyes locked onto his. There was something compelling about them, even behind a gold satin mask. Something fierce and ready. She flared and trembled in a pure, primal response. It was impossible, because what could it mean, this brief, hot contact? His float would roll by as the last had, and

Lisa would never know his face, or the man behind it. She'd never know if he sometimes wore a white mask and hood too.

But the next float rolled by and the next, each clamoring to be the wildest, the gaudiest, the most desirable of them all. Jess and Lisa piled trophy after trophy around their necks, to the glitter-eyed envy of the mob. What a world, where purple plastic beads conferred such a coveted and ephemeral status. The need and the noise surrounded Lisa, buffeting her: the need for the glamour of jewels, the need for pennies from heaven, the need for the mask, to not know who or what or why. The noise of a hundred hungers swallowed her. "Mister! Mister! Throw me something!" It buffeted her body and her brain until she echoed with it, until she screamed with the rest for more.

Her booty lay piled on her bed. It was lifeless now. No doubt some people would wear their necklaces out tonight. They'd carry the doubloons in their pockets and pretend to toss them, as if they were the princes of this town.

Lisa wanted to go beyond pretending. She wanted more than the illusion of escape. On this night of chance and abandon, she would abandon herself, her old sad self. She would not be lonely Lisa tonight. She would be someone different, someone not even of this world.

She wore a silver mask and a slink of a dress. She spread silver makeup over every inch of her exposed skin. She painted her lips and nails an icy blue. She painted blue spiral tattoos on her cheeks and across the tops of her breasts. The magic mirror showed her made anew; she was a shining being from a faraway star, a being made of light, of a metal strong and precious. Men might worship her, but they could not touch her. She did not deign to bring a coat when she left. Earth's dampening chill would not touch her either.

Promises was a madhouse. People screamed, knocked against, and groped each other, stranger and friend alike. Who could tell friend from stranger? Some were disguised. Most had been drinking all day. But Lisa's aura and appearance opened a path for her; everyone turned to look.

Jess did a double take. She grinned, waved, and dove back into the crowd, until all Lisa could see of her was a hand holding a tray of drinks above a sea of heads.

Claire wasn't there. They'd promised to spend the special night together. She hadn't called to say, when had she ever called to say, but Claire must be working late again. How long would Lisa have to wait for her this time?

The silver one would not wait. She would proceed. She would approach the bar for a drink. And of course the money she carried would be waved away this night by the bright-eyed bartender. She stood and sipped her drink. It was cool and smooth. If any of the nearby humans spoke to her, she took no notice.

The dance floor was a pulsing, bubbling mass of flesh. Above it, the disco ball sparkled and turned. How wonderful, if she could dance like that ball, high and steady and whole in herself. She hadn't danced in months. Richard hadn't danced with her after the first night, and there'd been no one since. No one she could stand being that close to—because no one came close to how he'd made her feel. She looked away.

And she saw Wendy. Sitting at the other end of the bar with Mike and some of his big shot friends, Toni sidling nearby. Lisa forgot herself; her jaw dropped. Wendy's eyes glittered dark like sunken mirrors. Her lips were drawn back over her teeth, in a laugh that made Lisa's skin crawl.

"Something bad is living inside that girl," said Jess at Lisa's side, noticing the direction of her stare. "And I don't know what to do. She won't talk to me. She won't see me. She thinks she's fine."

"Oh, Jess! Oh God, I'm so sorry."

Jess made a pained shrug. "Yeah. I just pray for her now. Hey, I got to go. Catch you later!"

"Sure." Jess left and Lisa watched Wendy. She watched those shiny eyes skip and slide across her, not seeing her, or not wanting to see. Poor Wendy! Lisa wished she could pray like Jess. Maybe there was comfort in it, but it wasn't real. Still, she bowed her head. And told herself she would not cry over the pain of this place, or she would never stop. This was not her world.

Lisa drifted toward the dance floor. She still didn't see Claire and she didn't want to see Wendy. She moved slowly, slower than the crowd required. Her head high, her steps measured, her surface bright, she moved slower still.

Inside her was a vortex, a whirlwind of emptiness. A perfect being was perfectly alone. In another minute her shell would collapse, and the din would crush her to her knees. She felt faint in the tainted atmosphere, and standing on this shifting floor.

A masked man was at her side. No, it wasn't a mask, but smooth face paint, purple and green, in a cover as complete as her own. He was well formed, this man. From what time and place did he come? It didn't matter. He'd come. He'd come, though she hadn't realized she'd been waiting for him until now. They turned to each other, the man and the woman. They created space in chaos, a pocket in the crowd.

His eyes burned. His mouth smiled. He took her hand. And she moved with him. Without any words spoken, without any warm-up, she moved with him. He moved, and she moved, like her body had been born knowing his. They danced close, closer than the crowd required.

They circled like twin stars. She was caught in his orbit. Bound to step when he stepped. His hands at her waist meant hers on his shoulders. He dropped hands to her hips and she set hers on his chest. He leaned forward; she drew back, though never more than inches away. He swayed back and she could not help but lean in. She was a captive of his gravity, swaying and pivoting around the white hot core inside her. The roar of creation sounded in her ears and the anxious voice of lonely Lisa could hardly be heard at all.

His hand cupped her bottom briefly; her fingertips stroked his nipple beneath his shirt. His thigh slid between hers; hers slid up the outside of his. He touched; then she touched. Everywhere, with most everything, except their masked and painted faces. They did not press cheeks. They did not kiss. They looked down at their bodies writhing in unison, and not into one another's eyes.

They'd moved deep into the dance floor. Couples shifting for the next song pushed them to the back wall. The man backed Lisa to the wall and ground his hips to hers. She felt his erection pulsing against her. She lifted and opened her legs.

Oh god, the fire, the core... she was having a meltdown. It blazed from her through him, from him through her. Her shell shattered, in a thousand tiny shards of light.

She felt him reach beyond her and push. The wall gave way. No, not a wall, but the emergency exit door. And he moved them through it.

They were alone in the alley. Though an overhang sheltered them from the drizzle, the cold damp air slapped and clung to her skin. Lisa held tightly to the man for warmth. The dripping all around her thrummed a soft relentless beat.

He smoothly settled his jacket over her shoulders. To protect her when he nudged her against the wall. He stroked up her leg, lifting her skirt. He stroked past thigh high stockings, past covered skin to bare. Then he hooked his finger and pulled her string bikini panties down until they fell at Lisa's feet. She stepped out of them. He unzipped his pants. Strange that his penis, engorged as it was, was nowhere near the purple as his face. But she still burned, and he must serve.

She flattened a firm hand over his heart and spoke once. "Cover it."

He dug in a pocket, pulled out a condom, and put it on. She watched the glitter dance of the rain, hot and cold like her. When he was ready and waved himself at her, she moved her hand. She curled it around his neck. She locked her fingers into his hair. She pulled his face into her neck, so his shoulders and the wet sparkling night were all she could see.

He gripped and lifted her bottom. She spread herself open. Her fire was deep inside. If no one reached it, it could die. She felt him poking, striving for it. She tilted her pelvis. She found his tip. She held her breath.

When he rammed into her, her breath leapt from her lungs, and he shoved her hard against the wall. She welcomed the shock, the lightning slamming her inside and out. He pounded; she thrust back. They collided again and again and again, a supernova blasting her into oblivion.

When it was over, she would have been less surprised if she'd found Richard in her arms. Less surprised than to know that her handsome, drunk ex-beloved didn't hold the key to her pleasure and release. She did.

The man withdrew. Tossed the used condom and zipped up. She picked up her panties. They were wet and dirty. She scrunched them up in her hand. She smoothed down her dress.

He held his jacket over their heads as they walked swiftly and silently to the front of the building. He held the door for her. She made a beeline to the ladies room. He made no attempt to follow. She would never see him again, never know who he was. She would never have to know.

Lisa sat in the stall, wiping and shivering. She wanted to laugh hysterically. She wanted to wail. She thought she heard screams in her ears, and the only thing strange about that was that the voice wasn't hers but Claire's.

If I Can't Have You

"I don't want nobody, baby," Claire sang along with the radio. She bounced a little in her seat, and tapped the beat on the steering wheel. It was Mardi Gras, she was finally off work, and rain or not she was ready to party. Driving away from downtown, the traffic was a piece of cake. She checked her watch. Damn it, she was still going to be late. She hoped Lisa wouldn't be too mad. But she had to change her clothes. No way was she going to get down and dirty in this staid skirt and jacket. Tight black satin pants, off the shoulder gold sweater, yes, much better. She pulled into her parking spot and raced up the stairs to her apartment. And came to a dead halt.

Stuck into the door with a penknife was a folded piece of paper. It was a tiny knife, almost a toy, but shiny with menace. She didn't want to touch it, but she damn well wasn't going to leave it in her door either. She yanked it out. She opened the note. It was typed and unsigned. But she knew who sent it. She read the words of his favorite poet.

> And when convulsive throes denied my breath
> The faintest utterance to my fading thought,
> To thee—to thee—e'en in the gasp of death
> My spirit turned, oh! oftener than it ought.

Jackson. Damn him! She thought he'd stopped harassing her. Well, he wasn't going to spoil her Mardi Gras with his morbid self-indulgent crap. She crumpled the note furiously. She pounded her fist on her door. Double damn him! She pounded again. But she didn't open her door. She turned and ran back downstairs to her car.

If she did nothing, he would stop harassing her permanently. Jackson was going to kill himself tonight. She remembered the two of them walking on the levee, an age ago it seemed. That was where he was, she was sure of it. He meant for her to go there and stop him. Or he meant for her to go there and watch him die.

Shit! Shit! Shit! She hated this. And she hated him for knowing that she would go.

She sped to Riverview, her car slipping and sliding on the turns. She cursed in time with her windshield wipers, and prayed that her anger would keep the dread from creeping in and the tears from pouring out.

She got out of the car. There was his car, the only other one here on this sodden night when all light and action were elsewhere. Claire ran in her pumps to the top of the levee, yanking her heels out of the mud with every step.

There he was, about 10 feet further downstream, standing by the water's edge. He was soaked through. God knows how long he had stood there, waiting for her, waiting to die. His hair clung in dark ropes against his white face. His eyes were pits of night. He held a revolver in his right hand.

"You came," he said. "Good. My final act should have a witness. Too bad you aren't a poet."

"Don't do this, Jackson."

"Why not, Claire?"

He mocked her. He knew all she might say — that life could change, that life could be made better, that life was precious no matter what.

He knew what she could not say — that she wanted him back and that she'd love him forever. She stared at the black holes of his eyes. How haunted they'd become. No. How haunted they'd always been, except for that brief time with her.

"Speechless? You're not going to say, for me? Don't do it for me?"

"Don't do it for me. Jackson. Don't do it for me." She took a step forward. She extended her hand.

Jackson said nothing. He looked away from her and out across the swollen river. He raised the hand that held the gun.

"Please!" He had to hear the break in her voice! He had to know that she meant it! "Please, Jackson. Don't do it for me." She took two more steps closer. She was only five feet away from him.

"But I am doing this for you, Claire." He turned back to face her. "Enchanting, untouchable Claire."

He smiled. It was colder than ice. She felt it freeze her blood and stopped still.

"Bewitching Claire. You always had the power. You could have saved me, witch that you are." He gestured towards her, waving the gun.

"No," she whispered.

He stopped smiling. "You could have saved me." His eye pits stared through her. "You were my last hope. But I've lost you forever, as you've made perfectly clear."

Jackson waved the gun. "You were so beautiful, so passionate…"

Hot and cold rain streamed down her face. "Jackson, please."

"I will never have anything so good again in my life. And if I can't have you…" He bowed his head. He took a deep breath. He stared towards her face. He gripped the gun and raised it. "Goodbye, Claire," he said.

She could not help it; she could not hide it. Mortal fear flashed through her. Not for him, but of him.

A terrible sadness crawled over his face. But she could not take back what he had seen in hers.

"Oh, Claire. No one knows me." His voice was as broken as gravel. "No one knows me. Not even you." He raised the gun higher. "I could never hurt you." He pushed the end of the revolver against his temple.

"No!" she screamed. She lunged for him. She saw him pull the trigger. The night-ripping blast tore into her ears and shredded his brain. Blood and bits flicked into her eyes. But she still saw him, his body flailing, falling, his half a head hanging from a neck all black with blood, his mouth gaping in a frozen scream. She flung out her arms, only to feel his thighs, his calves, his feet, slip through her hands. The awful sucking splash that followed took her soul with it.

She'd fallen on the bank. She scrambled up. She saw nothing but boiling water, flowing away and away and away. "Damn you!" she shouted. "Damn you damn you damn you!" Her knees gave way. She knelt, buried her head in her hands, and wailed. And felt like killing a dead man.

She had to stop. Her throat was raw. She had to tell someone what happened. He had a family. Oh God, oh God, his family. She'd never met them, but Eddie had. She had to stop. She had to find Eddie. She stumbled to her car.

Promises was a madhouse. It was still Mardi Gras. People gaped at Claire as she pushed through. They backed off. They backed away. She looked down at herself. She was filthy, her clothes caked with more than mud. But what difference should that make to them? They could go on with their party.

She saw Lisa come out from the rest room, and rush toward her. But there was Eddie. She tapped him on the shoulder. He turned.

"Holy hell, Claire! What happened to you?"

What happened to her, well, she wasn't sure. But what happened to her wasn't important for a change. "Jackson's dead," she said.

"The hell you say!"

Hell. Yes. And she had to say. "He shot himself. Down at the river. He blew out his brains and he fell into the water and got swept away. I couldn't stop him."

She told. It was done.

She collapsed, shaking hard.

Lisa caught and held her. She led her out the door and drove her home. She brought her into her bathroom. Lisa turned on the shower.

"I want to go to bed," said Claire.

"I know. But you've got some stuff in your hair. Here, let me help you get rid of these clothes."

The water did feel good, this hot bright water. It washed the dark away.

Lisa helped her into a nightgown and covered her with quilts. In her bed she was warm and safe. She heard Lisa answer the phone and the door. She was left alone. She had some peace.

All that was on the outside. On the inside, the black ice remained. She lay frozen, her vision frozen: the hanging half a head, the holes for eyes, the sucking water. Oh God, oh God, Jackson. God have mercy on your soul.

She couldn't love him. But she'd never forget him. He made sure of that. The tears she had for him were shards of ice inside her, below miles and miles of glittering dark water.

I Will Survive

The beveled glass of the door to Promises glittered with white fire in the black rain. Wendy wished she could stop shaking, but she'd done too much coke on the way over. Courtesy of her escort for the evening, her new boss, Dan. Dan was a friend of Mike's, and a rival bar owner. He wanted to show her off to him. He knew she hadn't let Mike come anywhere near her.

He opened the door for her. She half expected to see Steve inside. That would show him! But of course he wasn't there, and of course there was nothing to show. She'd moved out, they were over, and she was here with some guy she didn't even like. But what did that matter. She didn't like much these days. And at least he gave her drugs.

"Hiya, Joe," said Dan. Joe, the new doorman, the one who'd replaced Steve. Wendy didn't say hello.

The crush assaulted her. Why had she come? Dan led her through the pummeling crowd to the bar. He shouted out to Mike and Tommy and anyone else within range. "A bottle of Dom Perignon!" The most expensive champagne Promises offered. Maybe he figured he'd finally get lucky tonight, thought Wendy. And maybe he would. What did it matter? A few drinks and another snort or two and she wouldn't feel a thing.

"Wendy!" Mike beamed like they were old friends. "What are you doing with this loser? Come sit by me." He shoved the guy next to him off his bar stool and motioned for her to sit down.

She was glad enough to sit, even next to him. With her stomach clenched into a fist, it was all she could do not to puke. Her mouth stretched so wide it hurt. It wasn't smiling, though the guys seemed to think so. And the gasping sound she made at their stupid jokes wasn't laughter.

Her throat swelled; she could barely breathe. Her head pounded with blood. Her eyes were hard and sore. But she drank and she smiled and she laughed and no one knew, no one knew, no one knew.

They didn't know that this was hell. They didn't know that hell was exactly where she belonged.

Was that Dan nuzzling her neck? She shrank in revulsion, but the damned did not get to choose their punishment. She might as well enjoy it now, right? What was to come would surely be worse.

Oh god, she could still feel. She downed the contents of her glass.

"What the fuck!" exploded Mike.

Wendy stared where he was staring, where everyone was staring. At the normally elegant Claire plastered in muck, her eyes horror dark. She moved like a zombie, like the victim of a Voodoo curse. Wendy should be the one who looked like that, not Claire. She was the cursed one. Not Claire... This was wrong. Something was terribly wrong.

"What the fuck does Joe think he's doing, letting her in here looking like that?" Mike stood up. Wendy stood up.

"Hey!" cried Dan. "Where you going?"

Wendy didn't answer. She stumbled towards Claire. And got close enough to hear what she said. Jackson had pulled a trigger. Jackson was dead.

Wendy's gut wrung. She staggered out the door and down the street. She fell into puddles. She fell onto her hands and knees. Her stomach contents spewed through her mouth into the gutter. Her insides convulsed, again and again.

Jackson was dead. Really, truly dead. Why didn't she think of that? She should be the dead one, not him. Not him, not the baby... she should be the one. She vomited bile, thinner bile and then nothing. She heaved like she would never stop. Why couldn't she stop?

She couldn't stop because she wasn't dead yet. Not for real. She could stop if she were dead. Her stomach hurt. Her throat, her head, her knees... everything hurt. Everything was wet. And cold. Because she wasn't dead yet.

Not dead, but finished. Finally and fully hollowed out, she had nothing more to give up. She lay on the sidewalk. Raindrops tippetty-tapped on her empty shell.

She looked up at the sky. No stars to guide her. Just clouds dripping cold in her face. The raindrops sparkled as they fell. They were beautiful.

Got to Give It Up

Tonight the bar was wild. Jess had never seen the crowd so panting and heaving. She'd dressed for it too, wearing more on top than the pasties she saw on one woman, but not a heck of a lot more.

That was Mardi Gras. A time to let loose the bonds of normalcy, of decency — of whatever bond you'd got and didn't want.

"What ya got?" said Tommy.

She laughed. He was asking for her drink order, of course, not about what might bind her. As if anything could. She was a free spirit; all the guys said so. But she wished she felt as good as she looked. She was tired tonight.

"Red and water, two Cuba Libres, and a draft."

Quick as Tommy got the drinks up, Jess squeezed the limes and popped in the straws. And dove back into the crowd, holding her tray high. A hundred times she repeated it. She spoke a few words to a friend now and then, but the thirsty mob did not let up for a minute. She set herself to endure.

She wove in and around the flailing bodies, scanning for openings before they appeared, and before they disappeared. Then she felt a hand on her breast. She felt it squeeze, then pull away. It was no accidental brushing, nor a furtive fumbling. She spun around. Not one of the handful of men surrounding her looked different, either shameful or triumphant, from any other. They just looked bombed. Like whoever it was had already forgotten. Or like the invasive nature did not register with him, because that's what she was there for. She suddenly felt like slapping them all.

She went back to her station shaking with anger, telling herself to calm down. So what? So someone copped a feel while she wasn't looking. It wasn't the worst thing a guy had done to her. But then she'd gotten money for that. You don't get something for nothing.

Whoa. So if he paid, would that make it all right? No! It was not all right, not when she wasn't given the chance to refuse. She flashed back to the worry in her mama's eyes when she'd visited at Christmas. All the rest of her family exclaimed over her clothes and car and gifts, but her mama had gone quiet.

Tommy set a coke by her elbow. "You okay, Jess?"

"Yeah, sure. Just some stupid drunk." She shook her head and shoulders, shrugging it off.

"Yeah. I'm glad I got a bar between me and them some-times. You should be a bartender, sweetheart. Get off the floor. Be in charge. Be the top dog!"

The top dog went back to work. She should have but she didn't. She gazed down the bar at Wendy, who was laughing or screaming. Being on the other side of the bar hadn't helped her. Jess hadn't been able to help her either.

Suddenly Wendy and Mike and everyone near the front turned. Wendy fell off her stool and staggered away. What in the world? Jess shoved her way through the crowd, no longer dancing with it. Why didn't these fools get out of her way? It took forever to reach the front, to see what it was that had stricken her friend.

Claire! A drowned and broken Claire in Lisa's arms, and Lisa leading her out the door. Eddie stood in the space they had left, his usual smug expression wiped out. Jess fought her way through to him. These stupid drunken gawkers! As if they cared!

"Eddie! Eddie! What happened?"

"Jackson killed himself. I never thought he'd really do it."

"Oh my god! How?"

Eddie didn't answer. "I've got to tell his family... the police." He walked away.

Jess ran out the door ahead of him. Lisa's car was driving off. Down the street Wendy lay on her side on the cement. Rain poured down, dissolving the vomit in the gutter. Jess ran to her.

"Wendy, it's Jess. I'm going to take you home, okay? Come on, honey, get up. That's a girl." Her hands shook and slipped on Wendy's wet dress.

"Jess," Wendy whispered. Her eyes slowly focused, but her body stayed slack.

Jess wrestled Wendy into a sitting position. "Wendy! You going to be all right? Do I need to get you to a hospital?"

"No. No. I'll be all right." Wendy struggled to her feet. Jess helped her into her car.

"You just rest now, honey. And I'll be right back to take you home."

Jess marched back through the bar, water streaming off her naked skin. Tommy ran over when he saw her. He'd heard about Jackson. That wasn't the question in his eyes.

"I quit, Tommy. I can't do this anymore. I don't want to live like this anymore."

"Sweetheart! No!"

"Yes." Jess looked at him sadly. He was so gorgeous, and could be so sweet.

His mouth quirked into a sad little grin. "Well, I'll miss you, babe. You were the best."

"Oh, Tommy." Jess shook her head slowly.

"No. I mean, I know." He held out his hand. "I know what you mean. It's a crazy life."

She took his hand. She kissed it. She'd miss him, wild little boy that he was. She loved him. She'd never really thought about it before, but she did. She kissed his fingers.

"Why are you still in it then, Tommy? After so long, doesn't it get old?"

"Well, it may be a crazy life, but it's my crazy life. What else do I know how to do? Besides, guys don't get used up in it like girls do."

Jess let go. "Your heart does, though." She picked up her things, Wendy's things. "You'll never fall in love, will you, Tommy? Because you can't believe in love anymore."

Tommy hung his head. "I don't know, Jess. I just don't know."

Spring

Let's Go

"So, what's the occasion?" Lisa asked. "Why did you ask me here?"

Lisa and Claire sat sipping icy pink Hurricanes in the hotel's rooftop bar. Of course neither of them wanted to go back to Promises, but Claire's choice of this spot was unusual, though the view of the city lights and the black ribbon of the river was stunning. But since the hotel had something to do with her news, Claire thought this place was just right.

"The company is opening a hotel in Atlanta," she said.

"Yeah, I heard about that. Dale is transferring."

Claire remembered. Dale worked with Lisa on the front desk. His leaving wouldn't mean much, except that Lisa could quit having to turn down his advances. Claire knew her news would mean much more.

"I'm going too."

Lisa set down her drink and stared. "No!"

Claire nodded. "Yes. I've accepted a position there as housekeeping supervisor. In another year, I'll have had experience in every department in Rooms Division. I can be assistant manager next. It's a good move for me."

"You're leaving?" Lisa's voice was soft and piercing. But Claire was ready for it. She leaned forward.

"Lisa, come with me!" she urged. "I'm sure there'd be something there for you too. It'd be so great, going together." Claire laid her warm hand over her friend's cold one. She wished she could transfer her excitement as easily.

"We could explore the city together — find all the good places to eat, drink… find a new place for you to dance! And we'd get away from all the bad memories here." Claire paused. She'd get away, too, from the bad dreams, dark, sucking dreams. She snapped herself back. "Lisa, wouldn't it be great? Won't you come with me?"

"I don't know, Claire." Lisa pulled back her hand and hugged herself. "I can't believe you'd leave. I don't know what to do."

"Well, think about it, okay?"

"Okay."

"Good."

Lisa would come. She had to! Claire wanted it so. It'd be much more fun than going alone. But Lisa twirled her straw with her fingers and didn't look up.

Claire continued. "I haven't told Mother yet."

"She won't be happy."

"I know. She's like the Mafia. No one leaves the family." But her daddy had left her. Jackson had left her. Claire needed to go somewhere else too.

When her boss mentioned the position, she was struck by lightning. She'd never thought before that she could just leave. She'd never imagined she could change her life like that, and leave the city that was like family, that was everything she knew.

She'd thought that dealing with life meant staying with it. That's what her people did. They stayed in empty marriages, worked in family businesses they hated, then gossiped and drank and slept around. They stayed, and watched each other die.

She didn't want to do that anymore. And here she was, being offered another way. The company would help her. They'd pay her moving expenses, and let her stay in the finished rooms of the hotel until they opened to the public and she found a place of her own.

She had a way out. But she had to leave everyone she loved to find it. Her mother. Her brothers and sister. Even, maybe, her best friend. Claire's heart about swallowed her, but she bit it back.

"I have to go, Lisa," she whispered. "I can't stay. I have to leave before this place kills me too."

Lisa gazed into Claire's swimming eyes. "I know," her friend conceded. "I think I do too."

She's Gone

Wendy took a deep breath and knocked. She hoped Steve was home. She didn't know if she could get up the courage a second time. The door opened.

"Wendy!" His eyes startled, but immediately shielded. "What are you doing here?"

"Can I come in?" Her voice sounded small.

"Sure, I guess." He stepped back.

Wendy sat on their old couch. It was awful to see the walls so bare. He hadn't put up any new pictures. Steve didn't sit down. He folded his arms and looked at her; a frown knit his forehead.

She took another breath. "I came to apologize to you for how I left. I'm so sorry."

Steve lowered stiffly into the chair beside her. He looked at his feet. "You know, I'm sorry too. About... you know. I wanted to tell you. I tried to call."

She nodded. "I know. I wouldn't talk to you. I'm sorry about that too. I'm sorry about everything, Steve. Every bit of it."

A clock ticked in the silence. Wendy could feel the wall around him start to crumble. He studied his fingernails.

"Well," Steve said finally. "How've you been?"

"I'm better now. I'm working in a restaurant. Mostly elderly clientele. It's good. Quiet."

"Good. That's good." He leaned forward. His eyes held something in them now. A world of hurt, and a thread of hope.

Ah, if her heart weren't already broken, this would do it. She couldn't let it go on a second longer.

"I'm thinking of going back to Florida," she blurted.

"So... you're not here to get back together?"

"No." The word was full of tears. "We want different things, Steve. That hasn't changed." Wendy drew a breath almost as ragged as a sob. "And I'm better than I was... but I'm not good. I'm not whole. I don't know when I'll be able to love someone again. I'm still working on not hating myself."

She stood up. He did too.

"I just didn't want to leave things the way they were. I just had to tell you—it wasn't your fault."

Wendy kissed him on the cheek. "You're a good man, Steve. I hope you have a happy life. You deserve it."

She walked away from him. She drove away from his house. She did not look back.

She drove to the French Quarter. She wanted to revisit all the special places before she left.

She gazed up at iron lace, at brick fashioned before the Civil War. She peeped through gates, into slivers of secret jungle courtyard. God, it was beautiful.

And what was in Florida for her to go back to? Orange groves and housing tracts? Another scolding from her mother? Maybe she should keep to her original plan, go all the way to California, and see more of the world.

But she would miss this place, this deep and steamy place like no other on earth.

In Jackson Square, she saw the street artists, dreaming or working or talking. They were happy for a fine day this early in the year. Maybe they were just happy.

Down Pirate's Alley an old woman sat at a card table. She looked like Lola, but done up in head scarf, hoop earrings, and heavy makeup. No customer was at her table, so the woman turned the cards over for herself. She talked to herself too, like Lola did. Wendy drew nearer, curious.

The first card showed a nude woman kneeling by a pool. "Ooh, the Star! New hope, and blessings from Heaven. Ooh, I like that!"

There are nude women in Heaven? Wendy wondered. Whose Heaven was that? But the image looked more innocent than titillating. Maybe that was the point. Being free. Pure. Feeling unashamed. Wendy put her hand to her heart. She would like that too. She took another step closer.

The fortune-teller turned another card. This one showed two wretched people in the snow, outside a church window.

"Five of Pentacles, hard times. Oh no, I don't like that one at all. We've already done enough of that one."

The old woman picked up the card and put it back in the deck. She pulled another, of Grecian women dancing. "The Three of Cups, a celebration with friends. Oh yes. That's much better."

She looked straight up at Wendy and winked. "Sometimes, dearie, you have to make your own fortune." She cackled like a child.

Wendy jumped, but she smiled back. "I think you're right."

She dug in her pocket and handed the reader the ten-dollar bill she found there. "Thank you," said Wendy. "I will."

Celebrating with friends. She did have friends. Jess. And Lisa. She'd invite them over, that's what she'd do. Claire, too, if she was still in town. She'd had her apartment for months and never had anyone over. Never moved in, really. And it was time. Time she picked up a brush. Time she hung a few new pictures on the walls. "Thank you, Lola," she whispered.

The fortune-teller cackled again. "I don't know why you young girls call me Lola. You sure are funny little things."

Wendy stared.

But the woman turned her back, hunched over, and shut her out. She did not look up again. She turned over cards, chuckling softly to herself. "Funny," she whispered, "Funny little things…"

Good Times

Jess smelled like hamburger grease. She was so tired from her shift at the diner; she'd flop right into bed, but didn't want to stink up her sheets. She stripped, kicked her uniform into a corner, and stepped into the shower.

It was nice of the folks at the diner to take her back on a moment's notice, but she couldn't serve burgers all her life. The job went nowhere and would never end. Plate after plate, and change tossed into a jar. Though the customers weren't drunk and craving, it was still too much like working in the bar.

She had to think of something else to do; she knew it. She didn't come to the city for this. But she was just too tired right now.

She let the hot water pour down her, and wash her tension away. Too bad Tommy wasn't here to scrub her back. They used to love showering together. She heard his voice in her head. "You need to be in charge, babe."

He was right. She had to be in charge of her body and her life. She would not spend both of them going nowhere.

Sufficiently steamed, Jess got out, dried off with a fluffy towel, and slipped on a silk robe. She felt the fabric and sighed happily. At least she still had some of the goodies left from her former life. She stretched out on her satin bed and groaned deep and long.

The one good thing about being so tired was the incredible rush of relief when she finally lay down. It was near orgasmic.

The phone rang. Jess rolled lazily over and picked it up.

"Hello?"

"Jess? Jess? This is Neil."

"Hi Neil." Jess closed her eyes and forbore to sigh. She waited until he was ready to speak. She almost saw him rubbing his toe into the ground, worrying on what to say.

"I never see you at Promises anymore. Tommy told me you quit."

"That's right. I did."

"Does that mean you won't go out with me next Thursday afternoon?"

"I can't, honey. I work Thursday afternoons now."

There was a long silence. She held the phone away so he wouldn't hear her deep and uncontrollable yawn. But Jess would not build the bridge for him, not this time. Neil had to say what was on his mind.

She heard the breaking in his voice before she heard the words. "Does it mean you won't go out with me ever again?"

Shoot. However strange the relationship, Neil was a friend. A weird, rich friend. What was she going to do with him?

"I don't know, Neil." She couldn't think of anything else to say.

"Don't say that! Please, Jess. Please!"

Jess flipped around and put her aching feet up on her headboard. Fifteen inches above your heart for fifteen minutes was supposed to prevent varicose veins.

"Oh Neil." This time she did sigh. "Can you call me back later? I'm sorry, honey. I'm just too tired to talk right now."

"Later like tonight?"

Jess had to smile. "Later like tomorrow."

"Okay, Jess. I'll call you tomorrow."

"Bye, Neil."

She half sat up and stretched to hang up the phone. When she flopped back down, her robe fell open.

She looked at her body. Her tired, aching body. Her aching, lonely body.

She wanted to be touched. She missed being touched, held, loved, even if just for one night. She stroked her breasts. She thought of Tommy. She thought of him standing behind her, stroking her; she thought of his erection poking between her butt cheeks. She ached harder. Horny didn't begin to describe it.

Damn! She wanted him. But she wasn't ready to call him yet. Him, or any other lover, she said to herself.

Where was her vibrator? A quick release would do for now. Something easy. Then she could get some sleep.

She pulled her feet back beneath her. She searched in the pillows. She searched in the nightstand. She didn't find it.

Double Damn! She remembered the last time she'd used it, in the back seat of Gary's car. It was probably there still.

Jess smacked a fist into a pillow. She could order another from a magazine and wait six to eight weeks for delivery in a plain brown wrapper. Or go to the adult store, although the proprietor had a stare that was flesh eating.

Sex toys should be no big deal in this liberated era. Getting them shouldn't make her feel sleazy or dirty, when they were made for fun. She should be able to buy them where she bought other things for sex or romance. Like the sheets that made her sigh when she slid into her bed. Or the lace that she wore. The old postcards. The scented oils. The wide Chinese brush made of rabbit fur that she didn't use for paint. So many clever little things, bought here or there or there. People should be able to get this stuff out in the open. They'd be happier if they were having more fun with their sex.

Wouldn't that be great? Jess could just see it. A boudoir store like a jewel box, glamorous enough so uptown matrons would shop there, feeling risqué as they did so, remembering or imagining their younger days. But hip enough for the brave and trendy girls. A boutique of seduction. A place, maybe, to take a special date.

Jess oiled her hands and stroked herself and imagined giving Tommy a private fashion show in one of the changing rooms. She'd try on black lace merry widow after sheer pink babydoll, oh yes, watching to see what turned him on the most. She'd touch herself like she was doing now and watch him get bigger and harder. Until he was hard enough and she was wet enough and then she'd straddle him in his chair and rub his rod up and down with her body and rub her nipples against his chest, his cheek, his mouth. Until... until... she had him pierce her and she bore down on that gorgeous stiff length. In front of the dressing room mirror, they would fuck so hard they screamed.

Oh! Oh, wow! She caught her bottom lip between her teeth as she came. Wow. That was good.

Sex was good. Why couldn't everybody see that?

She laughed out loud.

She could open that store! Maybe not allow sex in the dressing rooms though; she didn't want it to be a place for the pros, since they had places of their own. Maybe that part would be just for her.

New Orleans was ripe for a shop like this and just didn't know it yet. All she needed was start-up money, but with several potential investors in her address book, that shouldn't be a problem. One of them, in fact, would be calling her tomorrow. And she, or he, could call others.

Not only investors. Maybe even a partner. So she didn't have to do this alone. Tommy? The ladies loved him, and guys could talk to him. More than that, though, he was smart as a whip. Tommy. Hound though he was, she wanted him. He'd make a fine partner, if she could just get him away from that damn bar. Getting him away, though, could take some doing.

Jessalyn's smile grew long and luxurious as she began to imagine it. Tommy, her, and all the different things she'd try to get him to come to her.

It Only Takes a Minute, Girl

Antoine's Restaurant. The letters were bold beneath the wrought iron rails of a balcony impossibly delicate and hard. Claire had insisted they come. "We can't possibly leave New Orleans without having dinner at Antoine's." The buildings on the Rue Saint Louis were close, old, and painfully pretty. Lisa gasped at the pang that shot through her. She longed, suddenly and sharply, for the simple presence of the prairie beneath a wide open sky. Instead of this… this carbuncle excreted by a sanguinary swamp. Lisa shook her head. It wasn't the city's fault she wasn't looking forward to this dinner. She grit her teeth into a smile and followed her best friend through the door.

She waited to tell her until after they'd been served, until she'd managed at least a bite of her trout meuniere. "I'm not going to Atlanta with you, Claire."

"Why not?" Claire demanded.

"Because for you it's moving on to a new life. Leaving your hometown, climbing the corporate ladder... You have an opportunity you're excited about, and I'm glad for you."

"Thanks, sugar."

"But for me, well, going to Atlanta wouldn't be a new life. It would be... just following you."

"You can make a new life for you too."

Lisa held up her hand before Claire could say more. "No, I can't."

Claire shook her head, still silently rejecting.

"Claire, you live and breathe Southern hospitality. You love the hotel business. You like the people and you like solving the problems. And that's great. But I don't like it. I hate everything about my job except for you. And that's not enough." Lisa set down her fork, not pretending to eat anymore. Waiters bustled, dishes clattered, and the ceiling fans slowly turned round.

"You don't have to work at the hotel. We can still spend time together."

"Claire. Really. I would only go to Atlanta for you..." Lisa's voice caught, and she paused a moment. "Only to see you get taken up and taken away by your job and your responsibilities. You know it will happen. And I just can't do it."

Lisa closed her eyes, remembering last night's decision, and last night's pain. Remembering Claire — the hundred kinds of laughter and the moments of unspeakable bond. Her eyes, her mouth, her elegant hands. Remembering as well the wretched disappointments, the tiny betrayals. Claire wasn't just leaving now; it was like she had been leaving Lisa for months. Lisa had to face it. She'd never mean to Claire what Claire meant to her.

Lisa coughed and continued. "You know the hotel could transfer you again in another year. You could go someplace completely different. The business is like that."

Claire joked a little. "That's one of its charms!"

Lisa smiled back. It was just like Claire to try to lighten the mood. "For you, maybe. But I... I want something more." I want to matter more to someone than a job does, was what Lisa didn't say. I want to matter more than a bottle. I want to matter. "I don't know what, or where I'll find it. But I know it's not in Atlanta." Not in another hot Southern city of fiery women and drowning men. She needed clear air and firm land.

"Well, I have to say I'm disappointed."

Lisa looked at the hands in her lap.

"But I guess I'm not surprised." Claire patted Lisa's arm. "You know I'm not so good at writing, but I'll call. I know we'll keep in touch."

"Sure," Lisa said slowly. "We'll keep in touch."

Claire continued to talk through the meal. Lisa half listened, half ate, and drank too much. She had hoped she'd feel better after telling Claire of her decision. But as

Claire planned, Lisa sank further. What was she going to do?

The waiter lit the liqueur of their Crepes Suzette. The flames leapt and she burst.

"Oh, Claire! What am I going to do?"

The waiter served deftly and disappeared.

"You should do what you love, sugar."

"What would that be?"

"You love to dance," Claire said.

"But…" But dancing was her way to deal with men, to play with love. Oh, no, not just that. It was music, it was rhythm, it was being in the beat, in the heart of it. It was being alive.

"But what?" Claire continued. "It doesn't have to be at a disco, does it? There are lots of different ways to dance."

Lisa stared, and then smiled, her first real one of the night. "Maybe dancing doesn't always have to be about sex."

Claire laughed. "But if you're lucky, it will! Takes two to tango!"

"Ballroom dancing?" Lisa giggled.

"Why not?"

"Yeah. Why the hell not?" Lisa lifted her fork in a salute, and took a bite of her dessert. The tangy sweet purely melted in her mouth. Really, why not? she asked herself. Claire was right. She didn't have to be in a New Orleans disco to dance.

She was suddenly sober and sure. She reached out for her water and knocked over her wine glass. Okay, maybe not so sober, but she was sure.

She would go home to Colorado. Her parents would give her money for college then. And colleges taught dance, lots of different ways to dance. She had a chance. She could learn a new way.

She'd go home to wide-open spaces, and people she understood. Even if she didn't like them, she mostly understood them. Which was more than she could say about the people here. It was more than she could say about herself right now. But that made home all the more attractive. Going back, she'd learn about Lisa too. She could "find herself," like the hippies used to say. And maybe someone who loved her, who would love her more than anything, would find her too.

Claire refilled their wine glasses. She proposed a toast. "To a new life!" she said.

Lisa raised her glass and agreed.

We Are Family

"Here's to us! Onwards and upwards!"

The four women in Wendy's apartment raised their glasses.

"I'm sure going to miss you two," Jess said to Lisa and Claire.

"I'll miss you too," said Lisa.

"Oh, I'll be back before you know it," said Claire. "Atlanta's not so far away. My family is here, and I'll come back for holidays."

"Good! I'd hate to lose my best customer before I even get started!" Jess teased. Then she said, more thoughtfully, "Do you think you'll ever live here again?"

Claire shrugged. "I have to see what it's like to not live here first. I can hardly imagine it." She shook her head. "But I need to. Maybe just getting away for a while, getting some perspective… But who knows what else might be out there waiting for me? Or who else?" She smiled and arched an eyebrow. They knew that look.

"Meaning Atlanta will have a whole 'nother crop of men to pick from?" Jess laughed.

"There is that." Claire coyly crossed her legs. She smiled. "Lisa will be able to pick someone new too. Right, sugar?"

"Right." Lisa smiled back. "I just hope I can find someone to choose, and who will choose me back."

"I know you will. You would never believe me when I told you, but it's like you shine. You shine with something… good. No matter where you are; no matter how you're dressed. It's how I noticed you from the first."

Lisa blinked at sudden tears. "Thank you, Claire." She cleared her throat. "Wendy, you're awful quiet."

"I was thinking about Lola," said Wendy. She looked up at the batik she'd finished and hung that evening. Lola's face, crisscrossed by lines, but smiling like Wendy had never seen her smile, with pure and simple joy, a smile she knew must be somewhere inside her just the same. "You know I thought I saw her in the Quarter? But I haven't seen her there since, and of course I haven't been back to Promises."

"I've been back," said Jess, "but I didn't see her there either."

"You went back? After you walked out Mardi Gras night? What did Mike have to say about that? And what in the world would you go back for?"

"Mike didn't have a damn thing to say. Nothing I paid attention to anyway. I wanted to see Tommy. Or rather, I wanted him to see me. To remind him, not just of the hot sex…" Jess paused to smile. "But of the friendship he's missing too. I'm going to take him away from that place." This was the part of her future plans she hadn't yet mentioned to her friends.

"Tommy leave the bar? You're joking, right? He's like a fixture there."

Jess smiled again. "We're going out on his next night off. On a real date! Probably the first official date he's had in years."

"I can hardly believe it," said Lisa. "Jess, you give me hope. If you can do that, you can do anything."

"Yep. And that's just what I have in mind."

The friends laughed. Tears might come later, when they were apart; but for now, it was a moment of pure joy.